'Martha Randa̶̶̶̶̶̶̶̶̶̶ ̶̶ ̶̶ ̶̶ ̶̶ ̶̶ ̶̶e from somewhere behind her, 'sto̶̶ ̶̶ ̶̶ ̶̶ ̶̶ ̶̶ instant!'

Martha swung round.

'I'm exercising my right to free speech!'

'Yes, and bringing disgrace upon the school! Get along home, the lot of you!' Miss Widlake made furious shooshing motions with her hands. 'You ought to be ashamed of yourselves! Behaving like a rabble!'

'There's no law –' began Martha.

'On the contrary,' snapped Miss Widlake. 'There are several laws. 1. You are obstructing the highway 2. You are causing a public nuisance 3. You are being libellous.'

'I didn't say anything that wasn't true! And we're not obstructing the highway, there's loads of room for people to get past. I w–'

'Right! You have now gone too far.' Miss Widlake breathed deeply, flaring her nostrils as she did so. 'I'm sorry, but you leave me no option.'

Always Sebastian

Jean Ure

RED FOX

A Red Fox Book

Published by Random House Children's Books
20 Vauxhall Bridge Road, London SW1V 2SA

A division of Random House UK Ltd
London Melbourne Sydney Auckland
Johannesburg and agencies throughout the world

Copyright © Jean Ure 1993

1 3 5 7 9 10 8 6 4 2

First published in Great Britain in 1993
by The Bodley Head Children's Books

Red Fox edition 1995

Printed and bound in Great Britain by
Cox & Wyman Ltd, Reading, Berkshire

RANDOM HOUSE UK Limited Reg. No. 954009

ISBN 0 09 930198 9

For Margaret Clark, who always wanted to know
what happened to Maggie and Sebastian

Always Sebastian

I

'**O**h, the idiot! The *idiot*!'

Martha was sitting in the kitchen wrestling with her maths homework when her mum's anguished cry came down the passage.

'Sebastian, you are an *idiot*!'

Sebastian? What was he supposed to have done now? He wasn't even here!

Urgently, Martha pushed back her chair and went racing out through the kitchen door, followed as usual by the dogs, all agog to see what the excitement was.

'Stupid, *stupid*, *STUPID*!'

The six o'clock news was on. Mum, who had been happily lazing about with her usual end-of-day sherry when Martha had left her, was now sitting bolt upright, one fist angrily pounding the arm of her chair.

'What's happened?' said Martha.

There was a tumbling of feet down the stairs and Sophie came rocketing through the door, pursued by Bigwig and Bunter, two of the cats.

'Did I hear you say Sebastian?'

'Yes! You did hear me say Sebastian! Always Sebastian . . . the *idiot*!'

The girls exchanged glances. Mum frequently got mad at Sebastian; he was the sort of person who got people mad. Martha supposed that when you cared passionately about something, as Sebastian did about animals, you were almost bound to get on the nerves of all those who only cared just a little bit, or even not at all. Mum cared, but she wasn't obsessed as Sebastian was – and as Martha and Sophie were. Mum always complained that Sebastian had influenced Martha and Sophie, and of course she was right, but Martha really couldn't see what she had to grumble about. The way Martha looked at it, it was far better to care than not to care.

'This time,' said Mum, 'he's well and truly gone and done it.'

'Done what?' said Martha.

'Planted a car bomb outside the Wellcome Labs.'

'*Sebastian*?'

'His mob.'

'The AFF? How do you know?'

'Because they said! It had all the hallmarks of the Animal Freedom Fighters.'

'That doesn't necessarily mean to say that it *was* them.'

'Or Sebastian,' said Sophie. 'Sebastian wouldn't do a thing like that. Though even if he did,' she added, 'it's no more than they deserve.' She snatched up Bigwig and cuddled him defiantly. 'They *torture* animals in that place. They deserve to get blown up, people that do that.'

'Unfortunately – ' Mum said it drily, in what the girls privately referred to as her 'have-a-go-at-Sebastian voice' – 'the only person that got blown up was an innocent baby in a pram.'

'Mum!' Martha dropped to her knees by her mum's chair. 'You don't mean it?'

'I'm just telling you,' said her mum, wearily, 'what they said on the television.'

'But Sebastian wouldn't do a thing like that!' wailed Sophie. 'He doesn't believe in violence!'

Mum pursed her lips. This was an old argument.

'He's not above setting fire to meat lorries and planting fire bombs in fur shops.'

'That's different! That's just violence to property!'

'Yes, and sooner or later someone was bound to get hurt.'

'But we don't actually *know* that it was the AFF. Do we? Not for sure,' said Martha. 'They always blame everything on them. And then it turns out to be the IRA or some other lot.'

'What conceivable reason could the IRA have for wanting to blow up the Wellcome Labs? It's very funny,' said Mum, 'that that's exactly where we were at Christmas.'

On Christmas Eve they had all four of them, Sophie, Martha, Mum and Sebastian, joined in a vigil outside the labs, in silent memory of the millions of animals who had suffered and died behind locked doors. But the vigil had been peaceful! They had flown white doves and read from people like Albert Schweitzer, the famous philosopher and medical missionary who said that 'until he extends the circle of his compassion to all living things man will not himself find peace.' There had been none of the shouting and fist-clenching that you sometimes got on the big anti-vivisection marches, when passions were inflamed and the angry chanting ran like wildfire through the marchers:

'No more torture!
No more lies! Every six seconds
An animal dies!'

Mum really hated that. She had approved of the vigil. Although she now worked as a therapist she had originally trained as a doctor, so no one could accuse her of just being sentimental when she campaigned against animal experiments. Vivisection, Mum said, was bad medicine. Sebastian – and Sophie and

Martha – didn't care what sort of medicine it was; as far as they were concerned people had no right to inflict torture on living creatures. They sometimes had heated arguments with Mum about it. But there hadn't been any arguments on Christmas Eve; they had all joined together, in peace.

That had been four months ago. It was the last time they had seen Sebastian because on Boxing Day he had had to leave early to get to a Boxing Day meet, where he was going sabbing. The girls had wanted to go, too, but sabbing was something else which made Mum nervous. She had visions of them being whipped by enraged huntsmen or thrown to the ground and trampled beneath the hooves of galloping horses. They could go when they were sixteen, she said; not before.

'I don't think,' said Sophie, resting her jaw defiantly on the top of Bigwig's head, 'that it's fair to blame Sebastian when he's not here to defend himself.'

'That's right!' Martha looked up at her mum, pleadingly. 'It's like not giving someone a fair trial.'

'Sebastian wouldn't *do* a thing like that.'

'He's always said, leave the violence to the other side.'

'Yes,' said Mum, tight-lipped, 'and you know very well what I've always said.'

One thing leads to another was what Mum had always said.

'First it's meat lorries, then it's fur shops, now it's car bombs.'

'But we don't *know!*' cried Martha. 'There isn't any proof! I thought in this country people were supposed to be innocent until proved guilty?'

'If it was the AFF who did it then he's as much to blame as anyone, whether he was personally involved or not.'

4

'I'm going to ask him!' Sophie tossed an outraged Bigwig on to the sofa and stalked across to the telephone. 'I'm going to ring up right now and ask him!'

'You'll be lucky,' said Mum.

It was a fact that Sebastian was almost never at home. He lived in a two-roomed stone cottage in the middle of a moor in Northumberland but spent most of his time travelling round the country working for the AFF. Mum said it was just as well or her telephone bill would be astronomical: Sophie would be ringing him up every day.

'The line's gone dead,' said Sophie.

'That's probably because he hasn't paid his telephone bill.'

'Or he's had the number changed,' said Martha, 'and he's forgotten to tell us. He was going to get it changed, because of being bugged.'

'Bugged!' Mum snorted.

'He was being,' said Martha. 'It was the police. You know the police bug people.'

'If people are going to go round blowing up babies then I'm all for the police bugging them.'

Sophie bit her lip; her face had gone all red. Martha could see that she was on the brink of bursting out with one of her injudicious remarks. At the age of twelve Sophie hadn't yet learnt to control her temper. She and Mum quite often had the most slap-up rows.

'I think,' said Martha, 'that we ought to wait till we know.'

'Know what?' said Mum.

'Know for sure who it was.'

Even if it did turn out to be the AFF, it couldn't be Sebastian. It couldn't be! Sebastian wasn't like that. Sebastian was gentle, thought Martha, going back out to the kitchen to continue wrestling with her maths homework. She had once asked him, 'Could you actually kill someone that was torturing animals?'

5

and he'd thought about it and said that he might be able to if he caught them in the act, but not in cold blood. Admittedly he'd added, 'However much I might like to,' but then he'd thought about it a bit more and said that killing the vivisectors wasn't the answer.

'We've got to keep up the campaign of harassment, but more than that we've got to make people aware of the horrors of what's being done . . . we've got to make them open their eyes and face the facts.'

Only a few people, according to Sebastian, were truly sadistic or callous or uncaring; the rest were just protecting themselves. They chose not to know what went on behind all the locked doors because the truth was too upsetting. It was up to the AFF to get in there and get the evidence: to bring it to people's attention so that they were forced at last to think about it.

Sebastian had been on lots of lab raids, stealing documents, taking photographs, rescuing animals. Mum always swore that one of these days he'd be caught, but he hadn't so far, though he'd been in prison twice for damaging property. He'd told Martha that when he was young he'd been too much of a coward to go on raids – not because he was scared of being caught but because he was scared of what he might see. He said the first time he'd broken into a lab he'd had nightmares for months afterwards. He said the horror never left you, but that for the sake of the animals you had to harden yourself and go through with it.

Sophie said that she would go through with it. Sophie was just waiting for the day when she could join the AFF and go on raids with them. Martha wasn't so sure. She didn't mind marching and leafletting, and maybe she wouldn't even mind setting fire to a few butcher's shops; but like Sebastian when he was young she didn't think she could bear to set foot inside a lab – to see all the poor suffering animals and not to be able to help them, because you couldn't possibly rescue them all. She really admired Sebastian for that. Even Mum had to admit that if it weren't for the AFF, and people like Sebastian, some of the very worst abuses that went on would never be disclosed.

Ben, the biggest and shaggiest of the five dogs who lived in the Randall household, came padding across the kitchen to lay his head on Martha's knee and gaze at her with loving eyes. (It was cupboard love: she was sitting next to the refrigerator.)

'It's only thanks to Sebastian,' said Martha, 'that you're here at all.'

Ben was one of Sebastian's rescues. If it hadn't been for Sebastian, he would have died a painful death in a cancer research lab. Mum had been cross when Sebastian had turned up on the doorstep with him – 'We don't *want* another dog! We don't *need* another dog!' – but of course she had taken him in. Sebastian always knew how to get round her. Their only really serious difference of opinion was on this question of what constituted violence. Mum was bitterly opposed even to the burning of empty meat wagons. If the AFF had really been responsible for this latest incident. . . .

But even if it were the AFF, it didn't mean it was Sebastian!

At nine o'clock they watched the news. The Bromley Bombing – they were already referring to it as the Bromley Bombing – was the first item.

'A car bomb went off earlier today outside the Wellcome Laboratories in Bromley. No one was killed, but a baby who was being wheeled past in a pram was taken to hospital with a cut hand.'

7

('Cut hand?' Sophie was indignant. 'You said it had been blown up!')

'The baby was released after treatment. A police spokesman said that the incident bore all the hallmarks of the work of the Animal Freedom Fighters. Local animal rights groups have recently been conducting intensive anti-vivisection campaigns against Wellcome and at Christmas held a twelve-hour vigil outside the laboratories. A spokesman for Wellcome was not available for comment.'

'There you are,' said Mum. 'Now they're dragging everyone's name in the mud. One incident like this and it rubs off on all the rest.'

'They still don't know,' muttered Martha. 'They're only guessing.'

'So who else would it be? You're not suggesting it's Monica suddenly gone berserk?'

Monica Bradley was the elderly Quaker who ran the local branch of Animal Action, to which Martha and Sophie both belonged. Mum didn't actually belong though she occasionally helped out at jumble sales or when an extra driver was needed. Mum approved of Monica because she said she wasn't 'extreme'.

'As a matter of fact,' said Martha, 'Monica isn't as opposed to violence as you think she is. She once threw a brick through a fur shop window. She told me.'

'She may have thrown a brick: she would never plant a bomb.'

'Neither would Sebastian!' shouted Sophie. She snatched up Bigwig and ran choking from the room. 'There are times when I hate you!'

'Yes, and there are times,' retorted Mum, as the door slammed shut, 'when I begin to wonder whether I oughtn't to have stopped Sebastian coming here a long time ago if this is the sort of influence he's going to have on you!'

Martha froze. She might be fifteen and more in control than Sophie, but there were occasions, none the less, when statements needed to be made. Martha made one. Slowly, and with cold dignity, she rose to her feet.

'I think,' said Martha, 'that I shall go to bed.'

'Why not?' said Mum. 'Do you good to get eight hours sleep for once.'

Martha tossed her head, swishing (as best she could) her long blond hair over her shoulder. Unfortunately Martha's hair was rather limp and didn't swish very well, but at least it would show Mum what she thought of her and her anti-Sebastian remarks. Mum was really mean to Sebastian; she didn't understand him the way Martha did.

There had once been a time, when she was Sophie's age, when Martha had dreamed of getting married to Sebastian when she was old enough – say, when she was sixteen. She realized now that that was just a silly schoolgirl fantasy, because how could you marry someone who was your mother's lover? She knew that Mum and Sebastian slept together whenever he came to stay with them. She'd known it even when she was Sophie's age and having her daydreams; she thought she'd probably always known it, even when she was quite little. She had memories of one Christmas Day when she had still been young enough to have her presents put in a pillow case and to lug the pillow case into Mum's room early Christmas morning, finding her and Sebastian all cuddled up with their arms round each other just like a real mum and dad. She'd said to Mum once, 'Why don't you get married so that Sebastian can always be here?' Mum had said, 'Would you like that?' and when she was tiny she would have done, and now that she was older she would again, but when she had been twelve she had wanted more than anything else in the world to marry him herself.

'Mum is so hateful,' grumbled Sophie, coming in to Martha's room to bounce on her bed with the cats. (The cats weren't meant to sleep in the bedrooms, but they always did. So did the dogs. Mum had long since given up the battle.) 'How can she think Sebastian would ever do a thing like that? He wouldn't!' said Sophie. '*I* might – but Sebastian wouldn't!'

'You'd better not let Mum hear you say that,' said Martha.

'Say what?'

'That you might.'

'Well, I might! If I got angry enough.'

'Yes, and you might kill someone that was innocent – you might even kill an *animal*.'

Sophie thought about it.

'That's why I know it can't have been Sebastian,' she said.

Next morning, the papers were full of hateful headlines.

ANIMAL TERRORISTS BLAST BABY – BABY HURT BY ANIMAL RIGHTS BOMB – THUGS THAT THREATEN OUR BABIES!

No one had any doubt but that it was the work of the AFF. Sophie had climbed out of bed early and tried ringing Sebastian again, but the line was still dead. When they heard the news over breakfast she said, 'All it was was just a tiny bit of glass,' but they both knew that that was not the point. It might have been more than just a tiny bit of glass: the baby could have been killed.

'Imagine how you'd feel if it were Bigwig,' said

Martha, only that turned out to be the wrong thing to say as Mum immediately jumped on her.

'Animals, animals! Never anything but animals! Just try thinking of human beings for a change!'

'We do think of human beings,' said Martha. They belonged to Greenpeace, they belonged to Friends of the Earth; what more did she want?

'Anyway,' said Sophie, still inclined to be fractious, 'what's so wonderful about human beings? They're no more important than any other creature.'

'That's right.' Martha nodded. 'You're just being species-ist. You're well out of date,' she told her mum. 'Modern thinking says we have to take the whole of the animal kingdom into account, not just man.'

'Oh, get off to school!' said Mum. 'I'm sick of talking about it!'

Because they belonged to Greenpeace and Friends of the Earth and cared about human beings as well as animals, Martha and Sophie always walked in to school. It took them nearly an hour and some of their friends thought they were mad, but it was a matter of principle. Sebastian never went anywhere by car if he could possibly walk or cycle or take the train, so neither did they. How could Mum say that he was a bad influence?

At school, it was Martha and Sophie who were said to be a bad influence – well, by some of the staff. Miss Widlake, in particular, disliked them. Miss Widlake was head of science and had crossed swords with the Randall girls on several occasions. One was when they had got up a petition calling for an end to dissection in biology classes and 520 pupils out of a total of 800 had signed it and it had been put on the front page of the local paper. Another was when Martha had stuck up large posters in the science lab saying RATS HAVE RIGHTS and Miss Widlake had complained about her to Mrs Kincaid, the Head Mistress. Vandalism, Miss Widlake had called it.

The latest clash had been when Miss Widlake had tried to organize a collection for the ICRF and Sophie and Martha had told people not to contribute because the Imperial Cancer Research Fund experimented on animals. Instead they had got up a collection of their own, for Quest Cancer Test, because Quest didn't use animals. Miss Widlake had been furious. She had accused them of sabotage.

Sometimes, in Bromley on a Saturday morning, Miss Widlake would come across Martha and Sophie handing out leaflets or asking people to sign petitions and she always went out of her way to come over and sneer at them. Once she had tried to argue with them in public about vivisection but Martha and Sophie knew more about the subject than she did because of listening to Sebastian and reading all the books he recommended and Miss Widlake had been worsted and had retired in a fume saying they hadn't the least idea what they were talking about.

'If you had diabetes you'd thank your lucky stars people had experimented on dogs!'

It simply wasn't any use trying to explain to people like Miss Widlake that the link between diabetes and the pancreas had been known long before Banting and Best began cutting up dogs, and that in any case the experiments had been useless and that one patient had even died as a result of them. Miss Widlake was a teacher and had to know best. Martha and Sophie were not her favourite pupils.

This morning, Miss Widlake was positively gloating.

'So it's happened!' she said. 'You've finally done it! Congratulations! I just hope you're proud of your-selves.'

'It wasn't anything to do with us!' protested

Martha, but everyone knew that she and Sophie had connections with the AFF, and everyone knew, because the papers were telling them so, that it was the AFF who were responsible. Even Ros Lawlor, who was Martha's best friend and had come to the Christmas vigil and met Sebastian, was inclined to be censorious.

'I don't mind them setting fire to meat wagons, but bombing a *baby* – '

'They didn't bomb a baby! It was an accident!'

'So who did they mean to bomb? They shouldn't be bombing *any*body.'

'People shouldn't be torturing animals!'

'Two wrongs,' said Ros, 'do not make a right.'

During the lunch break, Martha was called in to see Mrs Kincaid.

'This is a very terrible thing, this bombing incident,' said Mrs Kincaid. 'I'm not suggesting for one moment that you personally had anything to do with it – in fact, I should sincerely hope that you would condemn it as roundly as anyone.'

Here she paused and looked across at Martha for confirmation.

'Well, of course, I don't approve of car bombs,' muttered Martha.

'Meaning you do approve of some other sort of bombs?'

There was a silence.

'Fire bombs, perhaps? In furriers?' Mrs Kincaid shook her head. 'Violence is a slippery slope, Martha. I appreciate you have strong feelings, and I salute you for having them, but my dear, vio̶̶̶e is never the answer. I think in your heart you̶̶̶̶̶̶ ̶̶̶̶ow this. All I called you in for was to ̶̶̶̶̶̶ ̶ have the least idea or suspicion who ̶̶̶̶ ̶̶̶̶̶̶ responsible for this outrage, to spe̶̶̶ ̶̶̶ me or the police, it doesn't matter ̶̶̶̶

13

whatever you do, keep silent out of some misguided loyalty. A person who is capable of doing such a thing once is capable of doing it again; and the next time could result in tragedy. I'm sure you wouldn't want that burden of guilt on your conscience.'

Martha's heart hammered and banged as she walked back up the passage. Mrs Kincaid was asking her to shop Sebastian! *If you have the least idea or suspicion who might have been responsible* . . . But not Sebastian! Please not Sebastian!

At the end of the school day she met up with Sophie. They didn't usually walk home together. Martha was usually accompanied half-way by Ros, Sophie usually went off with a gang of seventh years. Sometimes they met up with each other; more often they didn't. Today they were both on their own.

'What's happened to your face?' said Martha. 'You look as if you've walked into a brick wall.'

'I had a fight,' said Sophie.

'Had a *fight*?' Kingdom House was an all-girls' school. People didn't have fights in all-girls' schools.

'I hit someone,' said Sophie, 'and she hit me back and we both got given five order marks and I *don't care*. So there!'

Martha didn't ask her what they had been fighting about: she knew well enough. Her little sister was notoriously quick-tempered, especially where her beloved Sebastian was concerned. Sophie had once had this fantasy that really and truly Sebastian was her father. For all Martha knew, she still had. It had made Martha mad with jealousy when they were young, because no way could Martha, with her wispy blond hair and blue eyes, be said to take after Sebastian. Sebastian was tall (like Martha) but his hair was still jet black even though he was the same age ᷑ Mum, and his eyes were deep brown, just like ᷑ie's. Martha took after Geoff Randall, who had married Mum while they were still medical students and been divorced from her five years later, when Sophie was barely a year. (He had gone off to America to make money and was now re-married and living in disgusting plenty in Los Angeles with two hideous spoiled American brats. You could tell they were spoiled, from their photographs.)

'You'd better not let on to Mum,' said Martha. 'You'd better say you were playing rounders and someone whacked you.'

'Why?' said Sophie. 'Why should I?'

'Because we don't want to upset her, that's why!' Surely even at twelve years old you had *some* sense? 'She's already fussed enough, without you going and getting yourself beaten up.'

'I didn't get beaten up. You ought to see Laura Hopgood . . . *she's* practically got a black eye.'

'Oh, God!' Martha groaned. 'That means her mother'll be coming round to complain.'

Laura Hopgood's mother didn't come round to complain (which meant that in all probability Sophie had been exaggerating) but the weekend was quite horrible enough without that. For a start Mum was all of a twitch and kept chasing across to the radio to listen to the news bulletins and see if anyone had been arrested for the bombing. Every time she chased, the dogs would get excited and chase with her, barking and tripping her up, which made her irritable so that she swore at them and cursed Sebastian for saddling her with them, and when Sophie remonstrated – 'They're only dogs. *They* don't know' – she turned on Sophie as well.

Martha couldn't understand what her problem was. What would it matter to her if Sebastian had planted a car bomb and got caught and sent to prison? When he was here she only nagged at him. Martha and Sophie were the ones it would matter to.

On Saturday morning they walked into Bromley to do their usual leafletting session with Monica and other members of the group. Animal Action were well known in the town, with their distinctive yellow tabards saying ANIMAL ACTION on one side and STOP ANIMAL EXPERIMENTS on the other. As a rule people were quite well disposed towards them; they came and chatted and took leaflets and sometimes made contributions. This morning, in the wake of the bombing, the atmosphere was hostile. One woman shouted at Martha, 'Murderers, the lot of you! Ought to be locked up!' Several people said they weren't going to give money for bombs to be planted. Martha was scared that Sophie would get into a slanging match and lose her temper. Martha had already tried explaining, in her meekest and politest manner, that Animal Action had had nothing to do with the bomb, but people were angry and wouldn't listen. In the end Monica said that Martha and Sophie had better go home.

'I don't want you girls mixed up in unpleasantness. Your mother would never forgive me.'

Sophie tried digging her heels in and saying she wasn't leaving till she'd got rid of all her leaflets, but to Martha's secret relief Monica insisted. Even Sophie didn't argue with Monica, though she grumbled on the way home.

'Sebastian wouldn't give in just because a few idiots thought he'd planted a car bomb!'

'You don't think he did?' said Martha.

'*Sebastian?*' Sophie stopped in her tracks, indignant.

'Well, if it really was the AFF – '

'*If* it was,' said Sophie. She set off again at a fast and furious trot. Over her shoulder, to the lagging Martha, she yelled, 'You're the one that says you shouldn't believe everything you see on the telly!'

That evening, on the news, it was reported that a

woman had rung the police claiming to be the person who had planted the Bromley Bomb – 'as an official act of terrorism on behalf of the Animal Freedom Fighters.' Sophie was jubilant.

'I told you it wasn't Sebastian!'

'It's still his organization,' said Mum.

'Yes,' said Sophie, 'but it wasn't *him*!'

2

On Saturday evening a week later, at ten minutes past midnight, there was a loud knocking at the front door. Beth and Buster, the two cross-collies, who had been snoozing on top of Martha's bed, instantly shot out into the passage, barking. Martha grabbed her dressing gown and tore after them, nearly tripping over Becky, the Jack Russell, and Bonzo, the white boxer, noisily erupting from Sophie's room. At the same moment, the door of Mum's room was yanked open by a long hairy arm and Ben galloped through. He was also barking.

All five dogs and Martha went bundling together down the stairs.

'Don't open that door!' Mum's voice called in sharp warning from the landing.

Martha stopped, her hand already on the latch.

'Why not?'

'You don't know who it might be!'

'It could be someone with a gun!' That was Sophie, dithering half-way down the stairs in her nightdress. 'They might shoot the dogs!'

'Ask them who they are – and shut those animals up!'

'*Quiet!*' Martha ripped the cord out of her dressing gown and lashed it violently against the banisters. The dogs looked at her, pop-eyed. Becky went on barking. '*SHUT UP!*' roared Martha, flailing at the banisters with her dressing gown cord.

The noise subsided. Martha put her mouth to the door crack. She felt a complete idiot.

'Who goes there?' she demanded, trying to make a joke out of it. 'Kindly state your name and business. And give the password,' she added.

A familiar voice spoke at her through the letter box.

'This is your friendly neighbourhood rapist . . . get 'em off, get 'em off! Knickers is the password!'

'Sebastian!'

Martha ripped joyously at the safety chain. Sophie gave a shriek and hurtled down the stairs. Becky tried to squeeze through the letter box. Ben turned in circles, Bonzo started barking, the collies sunk their teeth into each other.

'For heaven's sake!' said Mum.

The front door opened and Sebastian was instantly buried beneath a mass of dog. Fortunately he was only wearing jeans and a sweater. Sebastian never dressed up. Mum had once bought him a suit so that he could go to a special do with her and only at the last moment had he confessed that he didn't have a tie. He had had to wear Martha's school one. He had looked very strange, in a collar and tie; not at all like his normal self.

'Sebastian!' Sophie clawed her way through the dogs and unselfconsciously flung her arms about him. Martha wished that she could do that, but she had never been as outgoing as Sophie and fifteen was too old in any case. At fifteen one had acquired a little poise.

'What about Martha?' Sebastian disentangled himself and slung his duffle bag into the corner. 'Don't I get a kiss from her?'

Blushingly, she gave him one. She still couldn't sometimes *quite* suppress the romantic feelings of yester-year. She kept thinking she had grown out of them only to find them flaring up again as strong as ever. It gave her a warm, excited feeling deep in the pit of her stomach, but it was embarrassing, too, because it meant she couldn't behave normally with him.

'Well, it wasn't much of a kiss,' said Sebastian, 'but I suppose it will have to do. Where's Maggie?'

'She was there a second ago.' Martha turned, to look up the stairs, but Mum had disappeared. 'Maybe she's gone back to bed.'

'Did I wake you up? I was going to call, but I couldn't get to a phone box so I just took a chance. I hoped as it was Saturday you wouldn't mind too much.'

'We don't mind,' said Sophie.

'You don't, but Maggie might.'

'Oh, well! Mum.'

'Who's taking my name in vain?'

Mum had reappeared. There was something different about her, though Martha couldn't immediately think what it was. (It only occurred to her later: she had changed out of her old tatty everyday dressing gown, covered in cats' hairs and dogs' muddy paw prints, and put on the new red silk one that she had bought herself at Christmas 'for special occasions'. So far, there hadn't been any special occasions. Perhaps she had just wanted an excuse to wear it.)

'Hi!' Sebastian went bounding up the stairs towards her. 'You're not mad at me, are you?'

'Probably,' said Mum.

'Ah, mais Maggie! Sois gentille!'

Martha turned away. It was a terrible thing, to be jealous of your own mother. But it wasn't even as if Mum appreciated it, being cuddled by Sebastian. If he had folded his arms round Martha like that she would have been in seventh heaven – albeit as red as a peony. Mum just stood there, stolidly.

'I'll go and put the kettle on.' Martha headed for the kitchen, the dogs in tow. Sophie lingered, unwilling to absent herself even for a few seconds from Sebastian. Sophie, of course, was too young to be jealous, and anyhow she loved Sebastian in a quite different way from the way that Martha loved him. Sophie saw him more as a father figure. She would be shocked if she knew some of the dreams that Martha had indulged in.

They sat round the kitchen table, drinking herb tea and watching Sebastian (and the cats and dogs) devour half a packet of crackers and vegetable pâté. Sebastian always turned up starving because he either kept forgetting to eat or was too busy to do so.

'You'll never get to sleep on a full stomach,' said Mum.

Sebastian grinned. 'I hadn't thought of getting to sleep . . . not straight away.'

Mum blushed. She actually *blushed*. Sophie, getting hold of the wrong end of the stick (Martha had forgotten how naïve one still was at twelve), clapped her hands and cried, 'We could go out badger watching!'

'I don't feel quite *that* energetic,' said Sebastian.

'So what shall we do? Play games?'

'No,' said Mum. 'We shall go to bed.'

'But Sebastian s—'

Martha kicked at her under the table. Sophie looked at her, in surprise.

'Now what's the matter?'

'Just shut up,' said Martha. 'Monopolizing all the attention.'

'I'm not! I thought he wanted to do things. I was just – '

'Hogging the conversation,' said Martha. She turned, pointedly, to Sebastian. 'Sebastian, something awful happened the other day. We went picketing outside the Royal Marsden, giving out anti-vivisection leaflets, and this woman came out in her dressing gown and started saying how she agreed with what we were doing but it was the wrong place to do it because it was making some of the patients feel guilty, because of them having to take drugs that had been tested on animals, and do you know what she did?'

'No,' said Sebastian. 'What did she do?'

'She suddenly put up her hand and started pulling at her hair, only it wasn't hair, it was a wig, and she was completely bald because of chemotherapy, and she said, "Some of us in there are going to die," and it was awful, we didn't know what to say, we j–'

'We could always watch a video,' said Sophie. 'There's a new one out about factory farming. Monica's just lent it to us.'

'What would you have said? If you'd been there? Would you have argued with her? I mean, it was just so *ghastly* – '

'Compassion in World Farming. That's what it's in aid of. The video. I'm going to ask if we can show it at school.'

'Sebastian, what would you have said?'

'I'll get it out,' said Sophie, 'shall I?'

'You'll do no such thing!' said Mum. 'We're not watching horrific videos at one o'clock in the morning.'

'But we've got to watch it some time. And now Sebastian's here – '

'Look, just shut up!' cried Martha. 'I want to know what Sebastian would have said to this woman.'

'I think – ' Sebastian picked up Bonny, the smallest of the cats, and slung her over his shoulder. Bonny purred, loudly. 'I think I'd probably have told her that there was no need for anyone to feel guilty because if drugs were all that conventional medicine had to offer they didn't have very much choice in the matter.'

Sophie shrilled, 'They could always use non-conventional medicine!'

'They could, but if you're ill with cancer the chances are that you're frightened and you're going to do what the doctors tell you, and unfortunately most doctors are going to tell you to take drugs.'

'Yes, but you don't *have* to,' said Sophie. 'I wouldn't!'

'That's because you've done a lot of thinking about it. Most people haven't.'

'Then they ought! And they ought to feel guilty.'

'Oh, you're a hardliner,' said Sebastian. 'I don't have it in my heart to heap guilt on someone who knows they might be dying.'

'That's what we felt,' said Martha. '*She* wasn't there. Thank God.' She jerked her thumb contemptuously at Sophie. 'She hasn't learnt to have any discretion yet.'

'Hasn't learnt to have any compassion,' said Mum, 'from the sound of it.'

'I've got compassion!' said Sophie. 'I've got compassion for animals!'

'Why didn't you bring any?' Martha leaned forward to Sebastian. Quite often – *too* often, according to Mum – Sebastian turned up on the doorstep with a bundle of something that needed a new home.

Sebastian pulled a face. 'I didn't reckon Maggie would be best pleased with me.'

'You're dead right,' said Mum. 'She wouldn't! Now, will you two girls please get back off to bed?'

'Why?' said Sophie. 'What are you and Sebastian going to do?'

'We're going to bed, as well.'

'But Sebastian said he wanted to do things!'

Not those sort of things, you idiot, thought Martha.

'Actually,' said Sebastian, 'Sebastian's pretty

whacked. He's been hitching lifts all the way from north Devon.'

'Lifts in *cars*? Polluting the *atmosphere*?'

'He couldn't afford the train fare – and the cars were going to be on the road whether I was in them or not,' pleaded Sebastian.

'All the same.' Sophie snatched up Bigwig just in time to stop him consuming the remains of the pâté. 'It isn't very green.'

'So what do you expect?' snapped Martha. Sophie really was quite intolerable at times. 'You expect him to walk?'

'I can see I'm going to have to watch my step with that one,' said Sebastian. 'She's becoming a purist in her old age.'

'More fanatical than her teacher,' said Mum. 'I can do without two of you in the family.'

Martha liked it when Mum said things like that, including Sebastian as one of them. Days when Sebastian was here were special days; days she cherished during the long weeks, and sometimes months, when he was away from them. She wondered if this was one of his flying visits, when he came and went almost before they had had time to say hallo.

'You will be here in the morning,' she said, 'won't you?'

'You'd better believe it!'

'Will you be here Monday morning?' said Sophie. 'Will you be here Tuesday morning? Will you be here W–'

'I think what she's trying to find out,' said Mum, 'is how long you intend to grace us with your presence?'

'As long as you'll have me?'

'As long as *that*?' said Mum.

'As long as can be!' said Sophie.

'What's happened to the cottage? You haven't gone and got yourself thrown out?'

Sebastian *had* been thrown out of places on occasions, when misanthropic landlords had taken exception to him bringing back a succession of stray animals or letting rescued donkeys trample down the flower beds. Mum said it was quite understandable.

'*Have* they chucked you out?'

'Only temporarily. The guy who owns it wanted it back for a month or so.'

'What about the telephone?' said Martha. 'Sophie said the line had gone dead.'

'Yeah, I changed the number.'

'I said that's what it was! Because of you being bugged.'

Mum rolled her eyes heavenwards.

'She doesn't believe it,' said Martha.

'Maggie is a sceptic.'

'Only where you're concerned,' said Mum. 'Now, can we *please* all go to bed? We can continue the conversation in the morning.'

On Sunday mornings Martha and Sophie took it in turns to make an early-morning cup of tea – well, not so very early; no one ever stirred much before nine o'clock. This morning, after their interrupted night, it was nearly ten when Martha staggered down to the kitchen to feed the cats and put the kettle on. She was glad it was her turn and not Sophie's. She liked taking the tea in to Mum's room when Sebastian was there. It was strange that she never felt jealous seeing him and Mum together like that. Maybe it was because her romantic daydreams hadn't gone as far as actually getting into bed with Sebastian: they had always stopped at kissing. She wasn't sure about this bed thing. There were girls in Martha's class who claimed to have slept with their boyfriends, but as Ros pointed out, 'Sleeping with them doesn't actually mean *doing* things.' Martha didn't even have a boy-friend, or at any rate not a serious one. None of the boys she knew cared a fig for animal rights, and anyway they were all meat-eaters. How could she have a relationship with a meat-eater?

To her intense annoyance, just as she was about to take the tea up to Mum and Sebastian, Sophie came walloping down to the kitchen offering to help. Martha didn't want to be helped, especially not by Sophie. She had been looking forward to perching on the end of Mum's bed and having a quiet ten minutes to herself.

'I can manage,' she said testily, but Sophie could never take a hint. Twelve was really a very trying sort of age: old enough to believe (quite mistakenly) that you knew what was going on, young enough to be a stupid inconsiderate nuisance.

Sophie and Martha *both* perched on the end of Mum's bed.

So did the dogs.

So did the cats.

It was like a refugee camp.

'This is horrible!' cried Mum. 'I'm getting up!'

Before breakfast they took the dogs out. They usually walked for about two hours on a Sunday, but today, because Sebastian was with them and when Sebastian was with them things tended to get a bit out of hand, they tramped so far afield that they missed breakfast altogether and didn't arrive back till nearly two o'clock, by which time everyone's stomach was making loud rumbling noises.

'We can have blunch,' said Sebastian.

'It's not blunch!' Sophie corrected him, scornfully, in her superior twelve-year old know-it-all manner. 'It's *brunch*.'

'You can have brunch,' said Sebastian. 'I shall have blunch.'

'So shall I,' said Martha.

They had blunch in the garden, sitting beneath the

apple trees on rickety garden chairs round an old wooden table. The dogs and cats, as usual, joined in. There were no lines of demarcation in the Randall household, though Mum did occasionally go a bit mad when cats jumped on the table and stuck their heads into gravy jugs or dogs crammed themselves on people's chairs and tried to eat off their plates.

Today they were plagued by wasps; vast unseasonal hordes of them, dive-bombing the table.

'Off!' screamed Mum. 'Get away!'

'Don't slap at them,' said Sebastian. 'You'll make them angry.'

'They're making me angry!'

'They're hungry,' said Sophie.

'If we gave them something to eat – ' Sebastian picked up the marmalade jar, scooped a spoonful on to his plate and set the plate on the bird table – 'they wouldn't bother us. There you are, you see! Works a treat.'

'I do not buy marmalade,' said Mum, 'to feed wasps.'

'Now you're just being wasp-ist.' Sophie looked at her, reproachfully. 'Wasps have rights too, you know.'

'Not in this garden. Get that cat off the table!'

Martha removed Barnaby from the marge pot and let him lick her knife instead. 'Why didn't you really bring any animals with you? Haven't you rescued any lately?'

'Only a goat and I couldn't get it down here.'

'Thank God for that!'

'So where is he?'

'She. I found a home for her locally.'

'If you had brought a goat with you,' said Mum, 'or even a hamster, come to that, I should have sent you away with a flea in your ear . . . *I am not having any more animals*.'

There was a silence. Sebastian dug a finger into the

marge pot and offered it to Bigwig. Barnaby jumped back on to the table.

'We've got far too many as it is. It's ridiculous! The place is like a zoo.'

'It is not!' Martha said it indignantly. Zoos were horrific; the Randall animals lived lives of almost total freedom. (Too much total freedom, according to Mum.)

'If you didn't want pets,' said Sophie, 'you shouldn't have come to live in the country with a big garden.'

'That's right.' Martha nodded. Having a big garden was asking for it. What was the point of half an acre plus a small field if not to give a home to rescued animals? 'You should have taken a flat in Bromley, then you'd have been all right. Not even Sebastian could have foisted them on you.'

'No hairs on the carpet,' said Sophie.

'No mess.'

'No dirt.'

'You could have been a proper housewife.'

Mum picked up a pellet of bread and threw it at them across the table. Barnaby, seeing food go past, immediately stretched out a paw, knocking over a glass in the process. The glass, predictably, smashed to smithereens.

'You can't blame Barney,' said Martha, when Sebastian, without waiting to be asked, had gone back to the house for the dustpan and brush and swept up the pieces. 'That was your fault, that was . . . behaving like a *child*.'

'It's enough to make me,' muttered Mum. Fortunately, in spite of her grumbles, she wasn't in the least bit houseproud.

'Sebastian.' Sophied leaned across and tapped him imperiously on the back of the hand. 'We went leafletting last Saturday and people kept coming up and yelling at us and saying stupid things like we were murderers and we ought to be locked up. They're idiots, aren't they? One woman came up to me and said, "Does your mother know what you get up to?" As if I was peddling *drugs*, or something.'

'What did she say that for?'

'Because of the bomb.' Martha said it quickly, before Sophie could start off again. 'We kept telling them it wasn't anything to do with us but they just wouldn't listen.'

'Nobody listens. You can shout till you're blue in the face. I was telling Maggie last night – ' Sebastian glanced sideways at Mum: Mum's face remained impassive – 'it doesn't matter how many official statements we issue denying responsibility, the media don't want to know.'

'You mean it wasn't the AFF?' Maggie's heart gave a great bound.

'Since when has the AFF endangered life?'

'But I thought this woman had said – '

'We all know what she *said*. Or was supposed to have said. If there was such a woman.'

'You think they made her up?'

'It's not beyond the bounds of possibility.'

'A police plant!' shrieked Sophie.

Mum looked down into her tea cup.

'Whatever she was,' said Sebastian, 'I give you my word she was nothing to do with us.'

'I knew it couldn't be you!' Sophie flew round the table and wrapped her arms about Sebastian's neck, almost throttling him. 'I kept saying it wasn't! I had this fight with this girl at school – '

'*Oh?*' said Mum. 'I wasn't told about that.'

'No, because I didn't want to upset you. We got given order marks 'cause we hit each other 'cause she said all animal rights people were murderers. I couldn't just stand there and say nothing, could I?'

'Absolutely not,' said Sebastian, 'though I'm not sure you ought to go getting into fights.'

'But some people just won't listen to reason!'

'None the less –' Sebastian placed a finger on her nose, squashing it to a button – 'violence is not the answer. How many times do I have to tell you? Leave that to the other side. Right? Right! Let's get this lot cleared up and decide what we're going to do for the rest of the day.'

'I wish it were always like this,' said Sophie, picking up the tea cups and happily lobbing peppermint tea-bags into the flower beds.

'Like what?' said Mum.

'Sebastian being here . . . it's really nice. Just like a real family,' beamed Sophie.

3

'Sebastian,' said Sophie, 'do you think it's all right for people to ride horses?'

'Sebastian' – Martha flung her school bag on the kitchen table – 'we're doing this course for GCSE on animal rights and Miss Allmond s–'

'*Do* you?'

' – Miss Allmond said to bring in any material we could find, so I th–'

'*Do* you, Sebastian?'

' – I thought I'd take in a copy of *Freedom*. I d–'

'Look, shut up!' screeched Sophie. 'I'm trying to ask Sebastian if he thinks it's all right for people to ride horses!'

'Girls, girls,' said Sebastian. 'Or should I say women, women? Taste this.' He dipped a spoon in a pot that he had been stirring on the stove and pushed it at Martha. 'Tell me what it's like.'

'Mm . . . yummy! What is it?'

'Something I invented. Here!' He dipped the spoon back in the pot and thrust it at Mum, who had just come in. 'What do you think?'

'Nice,' said Mum. 'Is it for tea?'

Sebastian usually cooked the meals when he was staying with them. He was a better cook than Mum, who in any case didn't really have the time after doing a full day's work.

'Sebastian!' Sophie prodded at him, impatiently.

31

'You didn't answer my question! Is it all right for people to ride horses?'

'Well . . . horses weren't designed for people to ride on them, were they?'

'N-no, but do you think it hurts them?'

'Sometimes. If people are too heavy or they treat them badly or don't know how to ride them properly.'

'But if they treat them kindly? And don't overwork them?'

'*If*,' said Sebastian. 'It's a big if.' He took a dish from the oven and sloshed the contents of his pot into it. 'Why do you ask, anyway?'

'Well, it's just – ' Sophie sat frowning, spinning a knife on the kitchen table. 'You know I go riding? At these stables? Something horrid happened the other day. There's this new mare called Cara, and she's really beautiful, and Miss Vincent let this man take her out and when he got back he said she wouldn't move, he couldn't get her to do anything, and Miss Vincent said she was just lazy and when he took her out next time he'd got to be more firm with her, so next time when she wouldn't move he pushed her and yelled at her and made her canter, and when she got back she almost collapsed, and – '

Sophie knuckled at her nose. Martha could see she was on the verge of tears as she remembered the scene. Sophie was going through what Mum called 'an emotional phase'.

'It turned out the last place she'd been there was a fire, and her lungs had been damaged, and the dealer hadn't said anything, and so Miss Vincent didn't know and – '

Sebastian interrupted her. 'Why didn't she know? Who buys a horse without getting it checked out?'

'Miss Vincent doesn't buy them,' said Mum. 'She can't afford to, she has to rent them from the dealer. But she does look after them extremely well.'

'It sounds like it.' Grimly, Sebastian closed the oven door.

'She does!' said Sophie. 'Honestly! It wasn't her fault. She was just as upset as anyone, she got the vet in immediately.'

'Was the horse all right?' said Martha.

'Well – yes. But she won't ever be the same.'

Sebastian took his pot over to the sink. 'So what's happening to her?'

'Oh, Miss Vincent won't let people ride her any more. Not if her lungs have gone. She wouldn't.'

'So, I repeat,' said Sebastian, 'what's going to happen to her?'

'Presumably the dealer will take her back,' said Mum.

'And what will the dealer do with her? Foist her on to someone else?'

There was a silence.

'Sophie – ' Sebastian sat down at the kitchen table and took both of Sophie's hands in his. 'What do you think happens to riding school horses when they can't be ridden any more?'

'I – I don't know.' Sophie lowered her gaze.

'Have you ever tried asking?'

Dumbly, Sophie shook her head.

'I can tell you,' said Martha, 'if you really want to know . . . they get sent to the knackers' yard. That's what happened to Goldie.'

'*Goldie*?' Sophie's head jerked up.

'She wasn't the only one. There've been others.'

'But *Goldie*?'

The tears spurted from Sophie's eyes. Goldie had been an old mare, willing and gentle, whom generations of children, including Martha, had learnt to ride on.

'It wouldn't be so bad,' said Sebastian, 'if you had your own pony and were prepared to keep it for the

33

rest of its life, even when you'd outgrown it. The trouble is that people treat horses like commodities . . . it's too old, it's too small, I don't want it any more, let's sell it on and make a bit of money. They don't do that with dogs; why do it with horses?'

'Horses cost a lot more to feed,' said Mum. 'Plus you need somewhere to keep them.'

'We've got somewhere to keep them,' said Sophie.

'It's not only a question of keeping them for the rest of *their* lives,' said Sebastian, 'it's a question of making provision for them after you've gone. If you bought a young horse when you were fifty, it could easily outlive you. You've got to make sure it's going to be all right.'

'How?' said Sophie, eagerly. 'How do you do that?'

'Easy. You just put a clause in your will leaving enough money for somewhere like the Blue Cross or a horse sanctuary to take them.'

Sophie turned, breathlessly, to Mum.

'Mum – ?'

'No!' said Mum.

'If I had a field like that – ' Sebastian nodded his head towards the kitchen window – 'I'd start a mini horse sanctuary of my own. I'd keep rescued donkeys and ponies in it.'

'Oh! Mum! *Could* we?'

'I said no,' said Mum. 'We've got our hands quite full enough already – and *get that cat off the table*! I do wish,' she said to Sebastian, 'that you wouldn't go putting ideas into their heads.'

'Me?' said Sebastian.

'Yes, you!' said Mum.

Later that evening, when they all went for an after-dinner stroll with the dogs, Sophie said to Martha, 'I'm going to ask Miss Vincent.'

'About what?'

'About Goldie. I'm going to ask her if it's true.'

'It is,' said Martha, 'I promise you.'

'But why didn't anyone tell me?' wailed Sophie.

'You were too little. You were only nine. We didn't want to upset you.'

The tears came swimming back into Sophie's eyes.

'I thought she'd been sent to a rest home!'

'Well, she wasn't,' said Martha. 'She went lame and she was too old and she wasn't any use any more, so they sent her off to be murdered.'

Sophie turned a tear-washed face towards her. 'Did Miss Vincent tell you?'

'No, I heard her telling someone else. She said she didn't like letting it happen but she was running a business and they weren't her horses anyway. She was only hiring them. She couldn't afford to keep buying them just to save them from the knackers' yard.'

'But that's so cruel!' said Sophie. 'After she'd used them for all those years – ' Sophie choked.

'It's what happens to nearly all riding school horses. Sebastian says it's because we treat animals like machines, as if they're just put here to make money for us.'

Sophie blotted at her eyes with the edge of her T-shirt. 'Is that why you stopped riding? Because of Goldie?'

Martha wrestled for a moment with her conscience. She had been twelve when Goldie had been sent to the knackers' yard, and although it had upset her she hadn't at that age had such strongly developed principles as Sophie, perhaps because Sophie had always had the benefit of knowing Sebastian, whereas Martha had been four when her dad had gone off and Sebastian had come into their lives.

'Was that what decided you?' said Sophie.

35

'Well, yes, but it wasn't only that. Partly it was, and partly it just didn't seem right – '

'It isn't!' said Sophie.

' – and partly I just sort of lost interest.'

'I haven't lost interest,' said Sophie. 'I think I love horses almost more than I love dogs and cats – well, at least as much.'

'So go on riding them!' said Martha.

'I can't! How can I? Knowing that I'm just helping to wear them out so that they'll get sent to the knackers' yard!'

'Except that if nobody rides them they might just get sent there even quicker because people couldn't afford to keep them.'

'Maybe – ' Sophie said it soberly – 'maybe they shouldn't be used for riding at all.'

'Then they'd die out.'

'No, they wouldn't! There'd still be New Forest ponies and Shetland ponies and – '

'New Forest ponies are killed for pet food.'

'Well, then, people should only have them if they're prepared to keep them for ever, like Sebastian said.'

'Not many people can afford to keep them. You've just got to face it,' said Martha, 'horses have a raw deal. But at least they're not used in war any more, or for transport. At least riding schools aren't as bad as that.'

'Except when they send them to the knackers' yard!' cried Sophie.

Next day Sophie arrived home late from school, just as they were all sitting down to tea. She looked pale and tense and didn't even smile when Sebastian, hand on hip, mock camp, said, 'And about time, too! Another five minutes and the whole effect of my vegetable ragout would have been ruined. Completely ruined. Here I am, slaving over a hot stove –'

'Nobody asked you to,' said Sophie.

'Ooo!' Sebastian's eyebrows flew up. 'Get her!'

'Don't be so ungracious,' said Mum.

'Well, but he only does it 'cause he enjoys it. He wouldn't do it if he didn't.'

'How do you know?' said Martha.

'Exactly,' said Sebastian. 'How does she know? Here! Have some ragout.'

'What's *ragoo*?' Sophie stared down at her plate in distaste. 'It just looks like ordinary stew. Anyway, I'm not hungry.'

'Charming manners this child has,' said Sebastian.

Mum sighed. 'She's at that age.'

'I need a father,' said Sophie.

'You need a good hiding,' said Mum.

'Yes,' Sebastian nodded. 'I'm all for a bit of corporal punishment . . . Noël Coward got it wrong: it's not women who need beating regularly like gongs, it's children. Especially twelve-year olds.'

Sophie scowled. 'I thought you were supposed to be anti-violence?'

'Only selectively,' said Sebastian. 'Spare the rod and spoil the child, that's what I say. Maybe we should invest in a few whips and knotted cords. What do you reckon?'

'Fine by me,' said Mum.

Sophie scraped her chair back. 'You're just being *stupid*,' she said.

Sophie didn't go with them that evening, to walk the dogs; she said she had 'things to do'.

'What's got into her?' said Mum. 'Trouble at school?'

'I think it was me,' said Martha. 'Telling her about Goldie.'

'Yes, I rather wondered why you felt it necessary.'

'Mum! She had to know. Sooner or later.'

'Not about Goldie.'

'About what happens. She did, didn't she?' Martha turned for support to Sebastian. 'One can't go on for ever in ignorance.'

'One can if one chooses. But I think the very fact that she was asking proves that she needed to know.'

Mum threw up her hands. 'I despair! Why does this family always have to be so determinedly high principled?'

Sophie wasn't in the house when they arrived back. They called up the stairs and they looked down in the cellar, but she was nowhere to be seen.

'Now where has she got to?' said Mum.

They found her at the bottom of the garden, weeping as she poked at something in the incinerator.

'What are you *doing*?' shrieked Martha.

Sophie snuffled. 'Burning things.'

'What things?'

'All my horsey gear.'

'All of it?' Mum peered, aghast, at the charred remains at the bottom of the incinerator.

'All of it except the boots. I couldn't burn them,' said Sophie, ''cause they're rubber.'

'But what did you burn any of it for?'

'To stop myself going riding.'

'To stop yourself – ' Mum broke off, as if lost for words.

'That's a bit extreme,' said Sebastian, 'isn't it?'

'No.' Defiantly, Sophie smeared a smoke-blackened arm across her nose. 'If I hadn't got rid of it I might have been tempted.'

'You could always have given it away,' said Martha. 'Or sold it. We could have raised funds for AA.'

'But then someone else would have used it! Some-

38

one else would wear out the poor horses and get them sent to the knackers' yard.'

'Oh, Sophie!' said Mum. 'They don't all end up that way.'

'They do,' said Sophie, 'most of them.' Fresh tears started pouring down her cheeks. 'I asked Miss Vincent what was going to happen to Clancy 'cause he's got something wrong with his feet and she can't use him in the school any more and she tried to pretend he'd go to a good home but who'd want to buy a pony they can't ride? He'll go to the knackers' yard, I know he will! I've been riding him for three years,' sobbed Sophie, 'and I feel I'm betraying him, just letting him go off to be murdered like that! It won't even be kind, the way they do it, 'cause they treat them horribly!'

'No,' said Mum, 'I'm sure they don't. It'll be quite quick and painless, like when we had to have Bootsie put down.'

'It won't,' wept Sophie. 'Knackers' yards are like slaughter houses!'

'Tell her.' Mum turned, sternly, to Sebastian. Martha knew what she wanted him to say. She wanted him to say, 'Don't worry about Clancy, he won't feel a thing.'

'I'm sorry, Mags.' Sebastian said it apologetically. 'If I had to have a horse put down I wouldn't take him within a thousand miles of a knackers' yard.'

'You see? I told you! He's going to suffer dreadfully and it's not fair! After all the pleasure he's given people, and all the money people have made out of him, they just go and ch-chuck him away as if he's a w-worn-out c-car! You'd think the l-least they could do would be to let him end his days in a nice comfortable f-field somewhere!'

'Oh, *damn* you!' shouted Mum. 'Damn you and *blast* you!'

'Me?' said Sebastian.

'Yes, you! I don't *want* a field full of retired horses!'

'Oh, Mum! Just one!' Sophie turned to her with shining eyes. 'Just Clancy! Oh, Mum . . . *please!*'

'Sebastian Sutton,' cried Mum, 'it was the worst day of my life when I met you!'

Mum went storming off back to the house followed by Sophie hopping behind her like a demented duck. They could hear her beseeching wails receding up the garden: 'Please, Mum! Please say that you will! Oh, please!'

'I seem to have blown it again,' said Sebastian, 'don't I?'

'Wasn't your fault,' said Martha. 'It was mine, if anything, for telling her about Goldie.'

'Yes, but I'm the joker in the pack. If it weren't for me – ' Sebastian picked up the rake with which Sophie had been poking in the incinerator. Thoughtfully he clawed what looked like a blackened soup bowl towards him: it was all that remained of Sophie's riding hat.

'You know, I gave my word,' said Sebastian, 'I promised Maggie years ago that I would never attempt to interfere with either of you two g – '

He stopped. Martha blushed. Of course she knew that when Sebastian said 'interfere' he didn't mean interfere in *that* way; it was just that these days she seemed to have a mind like a cesspit. She had sex on the brain. Mum would be horrified if she knew some of the thoughts that Martha had about Sebastian.

She wondered, would Sebastian be horrified, if she were to tell him? But she would never dare! She would die sooner than let Sebastian know how she felt about him.

'That wasn't perhaps the happiest choice of words, was it? What I actually meant to say – ' Sebastian picked up the shell of Sophie's riding hat on the prongs of the rake and twirled it as he held it aloft. 'What I actually meant to say was that I gave Maggie my solemn promise that I would never under any circumstances indoctrinate you.'

'You haven't indoctrinated us!'

'I said I'd never try to influence you or push my views on you . . . and here you are, being shouted at in the street, getting into fights, burning all your riding gear – '

'Yes, but that's not your fault! It's not as if you've ever lectured us or preached or anything. You just made us . . . start thinking. That's all. You made us *care*.'

'You mean I influenced by example.'

'Well – yes. I suppose. But she can't blame you for that! We didn't have to be influenced if we didn't want to be. I mean, it was our choice, wasn't it?'

'It's your choice now that you're grown up. I'm not sure it can be said to have been when you were only little.'

'If Mum didn't like it,' said Martha, 'she could always have stopped you coming.'

'I sometimes wonder if that's what she ought to have done, instead of letting me keep disrupting your lives.'

'You don't disrupt our lives!'

'Yes, I do. You know I do! Always coming and going. Turning up unannounced – '

'We don't mind!'

'You might not. Your mum does.'

Slyly, Martha said, 'You ought to come and live with us all the time, then you wouldn't have to keep coming and going – well, not so much.'

'That would drive Maggie demented.'

'Why?' said Martha. 'She'd know where she was, then. And she'd like to have a man about the place to do all the things she can't do.'

Sebastian laughed. 'You tell me one thing your mother can't do!'

'Cook,' said Martha.

'Granted.'

'Mend the car.'

'Yes, but neither can I!'

'*Garden*. She can't grow things to save her life.'

'I can't see her putting up with me just for the sake of having a few flowers in the flower bed.'

Martha stood watching as Sebastian tossed the riding hat in the air and caught it again on the prongs of the rake.

'Do you know what Sophie used to think?'

'What did Sophie used to think?'

'She used to think you were her dad . . . I mean her *real* dad.'

Sebastian smiled slightly. 'Not guilty.'

'No, well, of course I know *that*,' said Martha, greatly relieved. 'But you see, if you had been she thought that you and Mum might one day get married and then we could be a proper family.'

There was a pause.

'*Would* you marry Mum?' said Martha.

'You're asking the wrong question. What you should be asking is whether your mum would marry me . . . I'm not really a very enticing prospect for marriage, would you say?'

'Why not?' Martha was indignant. When you thought of all those men who beat their wives to a pulp, or got drunk, or gambled, or went with other women, she would have said Sebastian was an excellent prospect. If she were Mum she would leap at the opportunity.

'I'm not what constitutes most people's idea of a good husband . . . no proper job, no steady income, no house, no pension – '

'I don't see why that should bother her,' said

Martha. 'She's already got all of those things. She's a modern woman: she likes having a job. She'd hate to be married to someone who expected her to stay at home and be a housewife. And she worries about you when you're not here. When you don't ring us for ages and you're not at the cottage, she really worries whether you're all right and what's happening to you.'

'She'd just worry even more,' said Sebastian.

'Not if you were married and she knew you were always going to come back here, so that she could look after you.'

'Look after me?' Sebastian twitched an eyebrow. 'That doesn't sound very modern womanish!'

'Why doesn't it? I don't see,' said Martha, 'that it matters which sex people are. If a person needs looking after – '

'Do I need looking after?'

'Yes, because you don't take proper care of yourself. Mum always says, "He's too busy caring about those blasted animals."'

'Someone's got to,' said Sebastian.

'So if you came here and lived with us, you could take care of the animals while Mum took care of you!'

Sebastian dropped the riding hat back into the incinerator.

'Somehow,' he said, 'I don't reckon your mum would go for that idea.'

43

4

By the time they broke up for the summer holidays, Clancy had been honourably retired and was living in the field. And because, as Sebastian said, it was cruel to keep a horse on his own, horses being sociable animals, there was also a rescued donkey called Amelia.

It was Sebastian who had found Amelia for them. He had a friend who ran a donkey sanctuary and was always looking for good homes. Amelia's story was a sad one. She had been discovered lying in a dilapidated shed, on a concrete floor, half starved and too weak to move. Sebastian's friend had nursed her back to health, and now here she was, in the Randalls' field, happily trotting round behind Clancy.

'You see?' cried Sophie, who still showed a tendency to burst into tears every time she thought of poor Amelia lying on her bed of concrete. 'It was the *right* thing to do!'

'I don't know about that,' said Mum. 'All I know is that it's your birthday and Christmas present rolled into one and don't you dare come running to me for anything else this year!'

'I won't,' said Sophie. 'I'll wait till next year, then we'll rescue two more!' She flung her arms round Mum's waist. 'You are the best and most wonderful and most darling mum on the face of this earth!'

'I'll second that,' said Sebastian.

'So will I,' said Mum. 'I begin to feel I'm in line for a sainthood.'

'And after all, there is always Martha's birthday.' Sophie turned, bright-eyed, to Martha. 'We could have another rescued donkey then!'

'No,' said Mum.

'Oh, but M–'

'I said no,' said Mum. 'I'm not such a wonderful darling mum as that.'

'But, M–'

'Now I mean it, Sophie! Don't push your luck.'

'It'll be all right,' confided Sophie, as she and Martha walked back together from the field. 'By the time it's your birthday she'll have got used to the idea. . . . Which shall we have? Another donkey, or a pony? You choose! It's your birthday.'

Martha didn't like to say that what she actually wanted for her birthday was money to spend on clothes. With so many abandoned and ill-treated animals crying out for homes, it seemed rather base. It was just that she had really been looking forward to going on a shopping spree with Ros and buying all sorts of lovely frivolous things like silver leggings and rainbow-coloured leotards and maybe, if she could find some that weren't leather, a pair of decent trainers.

'Well?' Sophie was jigging up and down by her side with impatience. 'Which shall we have?'

Lamely, Martha said, 'Let's leave it till nearer the time. I'm not sure Mum will agree.'

'She will if Sebastian's here!'

'Yes, well, he probably won't be.' Martha's birthday was months away. Sebastian didn't often stay longer than a few weeks.

'I wish he could be, don't you?' Sophie looked at Martha, wistfully. 'I wish he could be here *always*.'

45

'He says that would drive Mum demented. And he's not your father, by the way. I asked him.'

'I know that,' said Sophie.

Martha stopped. 'You *know*?'

'I've known for ages.'

'How have you known?'

'Found my birth certificate, didn't I?'

'You never told me!'

'I like to pretend,' said Sophie. 'I still pretend . . . I pretend Mum put your dad's name instead of Sebastian's 'cause it was your dad she was married to.'

'Your dad, as well!'

'Maybe,' said Sophie. She did a little skip. 'Maybe not. Now I'm not going riding any more I'm going to ask Mum if I can use the money she would have paid for rides to adopt some horses from Redwings. They've got this scheme, you adopt a horse and they send you his photograph and all about him. It's only £5 a year. I've worked it out . . . I could afford to adopt ten a month!'

At the beginning of August, Mum took two weeks' holiday and they went up to Henley-in-Arden to visit their grandparents, leaving Sebastian behind to look after the animals, also to build a shelter for Clancy and Amelia, to paint the outside of the house, to mend the garage door and to repoint the tiles in the bathroom.

'You're sure you've got enough to keep you occupied?' said Mum.

'Oh, ar!' Sebastian tugged an imaginary forelock. 'Thank 'ee kindly, ma'am!'

'He doesn't have to do *every*thing, Mum,' said Sophie, 'does he?'

'Yes! Everything,' said Mum. 'And if he has any time left over – '

'*Mum*!'

' – he can put his feet up and listen to some music.

46

What he *cannot* do is introduce any more animals while my back is turned.'

'As if I would!' said Sebastian, hurt.

'As if you would,' said Mum.

'You will be here when we get back?' said Sophie, anxiously.

'I'll be here,' said Sebastian.

'That was a stupid thing to ask!' said Martha, as they climbed into the taxi that was to take them to the station. 'You know perfectly well he'd never go and leave the animals!'

'I know,' said Sophie, 'but I just wanted to make sure.'

Mum at first had wanted to drive up to Henley; it was Sophie and Martha who had talked her out of it. Shamed her out of it, really.

'*Drive* there?'

'Polluting the *atmosphere*?'

'When there's a perfectly good train service?'

'It's people like you that should be setting examples!'

'Please note, I never said a word,' said Sebastian.

In the end Mum had decreed that if Martha and Sophie insisted on going by train they could both chip in and make a contribution towards the extra cost involved. Sophie hadn't been quite so keen then, because of wanting to use all her extra money to adopt horses.

'I suppose, as there are three of us – '

'The principle's the same!' Martha was standing no nonsense. 'It's still pollution whether there's three of us or just one. Cars are ecologically unacceptable. You know that as well as I do.'

The only concession Martha was prepared to make was a cab to the station – 'And *that's* only because there's such a rotten bus service.'

'What about the other end?' pleaded Mum. 'If we

got off at Birmingham International instead of New Street – '

'Cheating!' cried Sophie.

'But we could be there in forty minutes if Grandad met us in the car!'

If Grandad didn't meet them it meant going on to New Street, changing stations from New Street to Moor Street (carrying all their cases), then catching another train to Henley. It was undeniably far longer. And far more inconvenient.

'But ecologically sound,' said Martha. 'It's no good doing things by halves. We either do it properly or not at all. One has to make *some* sacrifices.'

They arrived at Gran and Grandad's a bit later than planned owing to a hold-up on the trains between Birmingham and Henley.

'Signals failure,' said Mum.

Gran tutted. Grandad said, 'If you'd let me come and meet you you'd have been here hours ago.'

'Unless there was a traffic jam,' said Sophie.

'Traffic jam? What are you talking about, traffic jam? We don't have traffic jams! This isn't London, you know.'

Sophie opened her mouth, indignantly. 'There was a traffic jam only last time we – '

'Quiet!' said Mum. She often had to keep the peace between Sophie and Gran and Grandad. Gran and Grandad didn't believe in 'all this new-fangled ecology nonsense. Lot of fuss about nothing! World's got on all right without it so far.' Martha had learnt to bite her tongue: Sophie still tended to retaliate. Mum had warned her, on the way up, *Don't* argue with your Grandad, you'll give him an apoplexy.' It was true that Grandad did sometimes turn alarmingly red.

'We thought,' said Gran, 'that as it's your first night we'd take you out for a meal. We've discovered this new restaurant – '

'The Water Mill. Only a thirty-minute drive – '

Mum's hand closed hard over Sophie's arm.

'Beautiful, it is – the most gorgeous setting.'

'Yes, and the food's excellent. Damn good value for money. We went there last week with Chris and Toni. They had lobster, we had roast duck – '

Martha saw Mum's fingers pinching into Sophie's bare arm.

'And all fresh vegetables. None of your frozen stuff.'

'That sounds nice,' said Mum. 'How are Chris and Toni?'

Uncle Chris was one of Mum's brothers. He was a financial adviser and was their least favourite of their uncles and aunts. Uncle Chris stood for everything that Martha and Sophie despised most: making money and acquiring property, with scant regard for the earth's resources.

'Just an ageing yuppy!' Sophie had once said, scornfully.

Uncle Jesse was their favourite, followed by Aunt Dot. Uncle Jesse was a doctor, like Gran and Grandad had been before they retired, but unlike Gran and Grandad he didn't blow up in a rage if anyone mentioned homeopathy or said that vivisection was evil. Uncle Jesse actually agreed that homeopathy might just conceivably have something going for it, and he was at least prepared to listen to the arguments against vivisection even if he didn't always go along with them. There was hope for Uncle Jesse.

Aunt Dot, who had also qualified as a doctor but had never really practised, was in fact a bit dotty, and furthermore had five children, which was at least three too many, given the state of the world's population, but the great point in her favour was that she liked Sebastian. Uncle Jesse was tolerant towards him, but Uncle Chris and Gran and Grandad became positively vituperative.

'We've booked a table for seven-thirty,' said Gran, 'so we'll need to be leaving about seven.'

Urgently to Martha, as they went to their room to get changed (Gran and Grandad being sticklers for what they called 'decent standards of dress') Sophie hissed, 'I hope this horrible restaurant has vegan food.'

'So do I,' said Martha. It was going to be bad enough having to sit and watch Gran and Grandad tucking into murdered animal without being expected to compromise their own principles.

'I'm not going to compromise,' said Sophie. 'If they haven't got anything I'll just have a plain roll and a glass of water.'

'But maybe even the roll wouldn't be vegan.'

'In that case I'll just have *water*.'

Martha knew as soon as they walked into the restaurant that there was going to be trouble. It was the sort of place with starched napkins and linen tablecloths and penguin-suited waiters wearing supercilious smiles. Gran and Grandad sailed regally across the room to a candlelit table in the corner. Mum followed, with Martha and Sophie trailing behind.

'Hey! Mum!' Martha poked her in the ribs. Mum turned. She smiled, rather nervously, as Martha screwed up her face.

'Just behave,' muttered Mum.

Martha thought, I'll behave – but I'm not going to go against my principles! Sebastian wouldn't, and neither would she.

They took their seats and a waiter glided up to them, proffering menus.

'Thank you,' said Grandad. 'Now, I'm afraid this trio are a bit cranky . . . they belong to the beads and sandal brigade.'

It was one of Grandad's little jokes: vegetarians always wore beads and sandals. And if they were men,

50

they had beards. (Even though he *knew* Sebastian was clean shaven – thank goodness! Martha hated beards.)

'I take it you do cater for cranks?'

'Yes, sir. No problem at all. Might I suggest the eggs florentine, followed perhaps by the cheese soufflé? Alternatively there's the cheese and spinach quiche. I can recommend that.'

There was a silence. Mum looked across at Martha and Sophie. Brightly she said, 'Well? Which will you have? Soufflé or quiche?'

Sophie stared at her, anguished. Martha said, '*Mum* – '

It was all very well for Mum, she was still only a vegetarian (except when Sebastian was cooking). She could eat eggs and cheese with a clear conscience, though Martha never really saw how. They had been over the arguments with her time and time again.

'We can only have *cheese* because the calves are taken away and *slaughtered*: we can only have *eggs* because most hens are kept in *batteries*.'

'And even if they're not they end up slaughtered.'

'Yes, when they've gone past laying.'

'And what about the male birds? *They're* turned into capons.'

'Put into tin foil.'

'*Eaten*.'

Mum knew the arguments but still she persisted.

'I think I'll have the soufflé,' she said, 'and the eggs florentine to start with. Martha? How about you?'

Martha swallowed. In a loud voice Sophie said, 'I can't eat eggs or cheese.'

'Can't eat eggs or cheese?' Slowly Gran lowered her menu. 'What is the child talking about?'

'I'm afraid they've gone vegan,' said Mum.

There was a pause, then: '*Vegan*?' Grandad, too, had lowered his menu. 'What nonsense is this?'

51

'We don't eat any animal produce,' explained Martha. 'It's really quite simple.' She turned, politely, to the waiter. 'If we could just have some plain vegetables – '

'You do not come to a three-star restaurant,' thundered Grandad, 'to eat plain vegetables! Choose something off the menu and stop being so pernickety!'

Sophie thrust out her lower lip. The waiter, trying to be cunning, said, 'Cauliflower au gratin?' He couldn't be so ignorant that he didn't know gratin was cheese.

'If we could just have the cauliflower on its own?' said Martha. 'And – and potatoes without bacon,' she added, rather desperately scanning the menu, 'and baby carrots not cooked in butter? And if we could start with avocado without any prawns – '

'This is preposterous!' Grandad slapped his menu on the table. 'If I'd known about this I would never have brought you here!'

'It's not very good manners, is it?' said Gran. 'Someone invites you out for a meal and you turn your nose up at everything.'

'I'm sorry.' Mum ran her hand through her hair, which was a bit more mousey than Martha's but also a bit more springy, to make up for it. 'I should have told you before. I was hoping for once they might bend their principles – '

'*Mum!*'

'Yes, all right, all right! I know. It's my fault.' Mum looked up, appealing, at the waiter. 'Can they just have vegetables? Would you mind?'

The waiter very faintly hunched a shoulder. Martha could tell that he wasn't pleased – vegetables, after all, didn't cost very much. But they *ought* to cater for vegans, she thought. She refused to be made to feel guilty.

As soon as the waiter had gone, Grandad burst out,

'This is crankiness run mad! Where are you going to get your protein from?'

'Grandad.' Sophie cast her eyes upon him, reproachfully. 'You're a *doctor*. You ought to know.'

'Sophie!' said Gran. 'Don't talk to your Grandad in that way.'

'Well, but Gran, people have been vegans for *years*.'

'Honestly,' said Martha, 'it's far healthier than stuffing yourself with animal fats.'

'Did you know, for instance,' said Sophie, 'that eighty per cent of bowel cancer is caused by eating meat?'

'Piffle!' said Grandad.

'Grandad, it's not! It's Cornell University. In America. They *said*.'

'You'll be under-nourished,' said Gran. 'It's all right for adults, if they want to make idiots of themselves. Not for growing girls.'

Sophie opened her mouth. Mum intervened, quickly.

'There's no problem with protein, I promise you. Or with anything else. I've looked into all that. It's just a bit inconvenient at times. When we're eating out . . . not everyone can cope.'

'I'm not surprised!' said Gran. 'It's ridiculous! You ought to know better, Margaret. I'm ashamed of you. You're doing them no kindness, giving in to all their fads and fancies like this. They'll grow up with all kinds of deficiencies.'

'As a matter of fact – ' Mum's tone was apologetic, but firm, Martha was glad to note – 'studies have been done which show that children brought up on a vegan diet are every bit as healthy as vegetarians and a great deal more healthy than meat-eaters.'

'What studies? Where? And don't blind me with statistics!' said Grandad. 'You know as well as I that figures can be made to mean whatever you want them to mean.'

'It's that Sebastian, isn't it?' Gran said it bitterly. 'He's the one that's put them up to it. It's a thousand pities you ever met that man.'

Martha, knowing how Mum hated it when Gran started on at her about Sebastian, said, 'Where did you meet him? You've never told us.'

Mum attempted a smile. 'I never knew you were interested.'

'Well, I am!' said Martha. She saw Gran and Grandad exchange one of their looks. (It was Gran and Grandad's opinion that Martha and Sophie were a great deal too forward.) 'Where was it?'

'In a house where I had a bedsit. Before I went to medical school.'

'And Sebastian was living there, as well?'

'In another bedsit.'

'What was he doing? Was he at college?'

'He was – ' Mum hesitated – 'waiting to go back to Oxford.'

'University?' Martha's eyes widened. 'I didn't know he went there!'

'Sebastian,' said Maggie, 'believe it or not, has a first-class degree.'

'Wow!'

'I always knew he was brilliant,' said Sophie.

'Brilliant!' Gran gave a little snort. 'Doesn't seem to have got him very far.'

'That's because he's devoted his life to fighting for animals,' said Sophie. She turned back to Mum. 'Why didn't you marry him instead of the other one?'

'If by the other one, young lady, you mean your father,' said Gran, 'then why not say so?'

'All right,' said Sophie, '*my father* . . . why didn't you marry Sebastian instead of him?'

'If she had,' retorted Grandad, 'you two wouldn't

54

be here and your mother would have ended up in a mental home!'

'Why?' Sophie sat up, truculently and straight-backed on her chair.

'Because the man's a lunatic!'

'Dad, please!' said Mum. 'Not now!'

'I'm sorry, Margaret, but this vegan nonsense really is the last straw. They're like Pavlov's dogs, the pair of them. Conditioned to do just whatever he tells them.'

'Grandad,' said Sophie, 'Pavlov's dogs were *tortured*.'

'Oh, don't be so stupid! Of course they weren't.'

'They were,' said Martha. She leaned forward earnestly across the table. 'He confused them and frustrated them and made them neurotic . . . it was *psychological* torture.'

'Poppycock!' Grandad's face had turned ominously red. 'I suppose that's more drivel he's fed you?'

'Yes,' said Gran, 'and what about that baby they bombed? The one in Bromley?'

Martha was about to say 'What about it?' when Mum kicked at her under the table.

'Sebastian,' said Mum, 'had nothing to do with the bombing. Neither did the AFF. The woman who claimed responsibility was not one of their members. Now, please! Everybody! Can we just stop all this and concentrate on having dinner? Why has no one offered me a drink?'

'Never know these days whether you've gone and become teetotal,' grunted Grandad.

'Certainly not!' said Mum. 'I should like a large gin and tonic.'

Staying with Gran and Grandad was never a very comfortable experience. Gran had become houseproud in her old age (not an animal to be seen) so that Mum grew nervous and lived in a state of constant fuss – 'Sophie, put a mat under that plate! Martha, pick those crumbs up!'

Grandad tried gallantly to keep them amused, laying on trips to Hereford and Worcester and even as far as Cheltenham and Bath, not realizing that they would have been far happier left on their own with a couple of bicycles. Martha was anguished about all the pollution they were causing and Sophie got car sick. Also, they weren't very good at looking at cathedrals, which was what Grandad mostly seemed to want them to do. Martha felt guilty, for after all Grandad was doing his best, but Sophie just grew fractious and whined about the heat so that Mum had to hush her up and sharply remind her that 'Good manners never hurt anyone.'

They sent cards to Sebastian and at the end of the first week Mum rang home, just to check that everything was all right – in other words, to check that he hadn't turned the place into a full-scale animal sanctuary in her absence. Gran was sour and said, 'Margaret's too trusting. She lets herself be put upon.'

'Who by?' said Sophie.

'How often does that layabout come and scrounge off you?'

Sophie took a breath: Martha jabbed her in the ribs. It wasn't any use arguing with Gran. Unlike Grandad, who went all red and apoplectic, Gran just froze, like an iceberg. Besides, it would upset Mum.

'We don't see it as scrounging,' said Martha. 'He looks after the animals for us. If Sebastian weren't there to look after them we wouldn't be able to come and visit you.'

'And anyway,' said Sophie, 'he's painting the house.'

Gran sniffed, but fortunately before she could say anything Mum had come back from the telephone.

'You two can have a quick word if you want,' said Mum, 'but keep it short. Think of Gran and Grandad's telephone bill.'

It was Sophie who needed to be told, not Martha. Martha always felt shy, speaking to Sebastian on the telephone. Sophie, needless to say, never felt shy with anyone. She would have chatted half the morning if Mum hadn't put a stop to it.

On their last Saturday, which was the day before they went home, Uncle Chris and Aunt Toni paid a visit. Aunt Toni was a computer programmer and rather high-powered. She always dressed as if she were about to go into battle. (Sophie, when younger, had once asked in all innocence why 'Aunt Toni wears coat hangers in her clothes?') Even now, in the middle of a July heatwave, while everyone else was slopping about in T-shirts and shorts, Aunt Toni was wearing one of her square-cut smartly-tailored suits, complete with coat hanger shoulders. To Martha's relief, after the obligatory hallo's and how are you's, Mum said she and Sophie could go off if they wanted.

'She knows if we stay,' said Sophie, 'things will only go wrong.'

'Especially if Uncle Chris starts on about Sebastian again.'

Uncle Chris had been at school with Sebastian. Last time they had stayed in Henley-in-Arden they had all of them, Uncle Chris, Gran and Grandad, ganged up on Mum and started lecturing her about how it was time she sent Sebastian packing, how Sebastian had ruined her life, how if it hadn't been for him she would have remarried years ago. Gran had even hinted that if it hadn't been for Sebastian Mum might never have got divorced in the first place. Mum had said, 'It's true that if it hadn't been for

Sebastian I might never have *married* Geoff in the first place, but he had nothing whatsoever to do with our getting divorced.'

Uncle Chris had then chimed in, 'The guy's a nutter, he always was,' at which point Sophie had said something rude and unforgiveable and Gran had accused Mum of bringing up her children to have no respect and Mum had lost her temper and Grandad had tut-tutted and said, 'Now then, Margaret! Now then, Margaret! Enough of that!' while Martha, trying to help but in fact, as she could see in retrospect, only making matters worse, had yelled, 'It's not Mum's fault! She didn't start it!' Everything had been quite dreadful.

'We're far safer out here,' said Sophie. 'At least this way we can't upset anyone.'

As Martha said later, famous last words. . . .

It was Martha who saw the dog in the car: it was Sophie who decided that the dog was suffocating and had to be got out.

'It's *criminal*, leaving an animal locked in a car on a day like this! Look at him, he can hardly breathe!'

It was true that the car was in full sunlight. Even so, Martha hesitated.

'Maybe we should just wait here for a bit and see if the owner comes back.'

'By then it could be too late! Sebastian was telling me . . . a dog *died* the other day because it had been left in a car without any shade.'

'Let's go and knock at some doors,' said Martha, 'and see if anyone knows who it belongs to.'

They knocked at several doors but it seemed that nobody was at home in Henley-in-Arden on a Sunday morning. Maybe they were all at church, or all in bed, or all away on holiday, but after walking half-way up the street Martha could still get no one to answer.

'I'm not waiting any longer!' said Sophie. 'He'll be fried to death if this goes on!'

Martha watched, apprehensive yet at the same time secretly relieved that the decision had been taken out of her hands, as Sophie cast round for something with which to break the car window. In the event, which was no doubt just as well, car windows turned out to be a great deal tougher than either of them had imagined: the heel of Sophie's trainer made no impact at all, other than to incite the imprisoned dog to a frenzy of barking. It did cross Martha's mind that a dog who could bark as vociferously as that might not perhaps be quite as far gone as Sophie had imagined, but before she had time to put the thought into words another voice had intruded upon the scene. It did not, on the whole, sound pleased. What it said, in decidedly chilling tones, was: 'Might I ask what you think you are up to?'

'Well, how was I to know?' said Sophie, aggrieved, as they made their way back to Gran and Grandad's. 'If someone's going to leave a dog shut up in a car in the blazing sunshine while he goes off and buys a paper, he ought to leave a note telling people. Suppose he'd had a heart attack and hadn't come back? Dogs can suffocate in *minutes*.'

'Just as well he knew Gran and Grandad,' said Martha, 'otherwise we might have ended up at the police station.'

'Needn't think *I'd* care,' said Sophie. 'I suppose he'll go and snitch on us.'

'Bound to.' Martha said it gloomily. There was never anything but trouble when they came to visit Gran and Grandad. 'We probably ought to warn Mum.'

They told her the story on the way home next day in the train. Mum took it quite philosophically.

'It'll just be another nail in our coffin . . . they'll blame it on Sebastian, of course.'

'Why are they always so horrible about Sebastian?' said Sophie.

'Oh! I don't know. Basically because his outlook on life is a million light years away from theirs.'

'Which do you prefer,' said Sophie. 'Sebastian's outlook? Or Gran and Grandad's?'

'I don't think you need ask that,' said Mum.

It was wonderful to be home again. As Sebastian opened the front door, all the dogs came spilling out in a joyous cascade of bark and bounce.

'Still only five?' shouted Mum, above the hubbub.

'What?' shouted back Sebastian.

'Five! Five dogs! I've been terrified I'd come back and find you'd given house room to half a dozen more!'

'No. Just the one extra cat,' said Sebastian.

Mum froze. 'What?'

'Cat. Someone brought it to the door last night saying it was a stray and they thought the "animal lady" would take it in. That's you,' said Sebastian. 'The animal lady . . . well, it can hardly be me, can it?'

'You didn't have to take it in!' cried Mum.

Sebastian turned. 'I'll go and chuck it out again.'

'Oh! Sebastian! No!' The two girls wailed at him in unison.

'Where is he?'

'What's he like?'

'Let's see him!'

Mum sighed as she closed the front gate.

'My mother is quite right . . . you are not to be trusted!'

5

Sebastian was with them for the whole of the summer. Every now and again he would disappear on mysterious assignments for the AFF which he couldn't tell them about – 'The fewer people who know, the better' – but in any case they had learnt by now not to ask. It didn't make them any less curious, or less anxious. Every time he went off, Sophie and Martha held their breaths until he was safely back with them again. They could still remember an occasion some years ago when he had promised to be present at a Christmas party only to end up in police custody instead. (He had been hunt sabbing and some of the hunt people had turned nasty.) Mum had had to go and bail him out. Sophie and Martha, though naturally disappointed by him not turning up for the party, had secretly thought it rather splendid to be arrested for standing up for your principles. Mum had been a bit short about it. She had seemed to think it was more shameful than splendid, not to mention grossly inconsiderate.

In September, the man who owned Sebastian's cottage in Northumberland rang to say he was going to be staying there longer than anticipated – 'at least until the end of October.' Sebastian relayed the news apologetically to Mum one evening over tea.

'I'm really sorry about that. I'd planned on getting out of your hair this weekend and leaving you in peace for the last couple of weeks before the girls go back to school.'

'Why?' said Sophie. 'We like having you in our hair.'

'We don't want to be left in peace.'

'It's nice having you here.'

Sebastian pulled a face and went on talking to Mum.

'I've managed to find someone who can put me up from next Friday. If you could just bear with me till – '

'Put you up where?' said Mum.

'His place.'

'It's not one of your dodgy animal rights friends living in some squalid bedsit, is it?'

'Well – it's a colleague.'

'In a bedsit?'

'You don't have to be so snooty about it! It's a step-up for him. This time last year he was in a cardboard box.'

'*Sebastian*!' said Sophie, shocked. 'You shouldn't joke about things like that.'

'It's no joke, lady . . . I'm serious.'

'So where is he planning that you should sleep?' said Mum. 'On the floor?'

Sebastian shrugged.

'You're getting too old for this sort of thing. Sleeping on people's floors is a young man's game.'

'Yes, you're too old!' said Sophie. 'Stay here with us and sleep in a bed.'

'You're beginning to make me feel positively ancient!'

'You will be,' said Mum, 'if you carry on like this.'

'I hope that's not a subtle hint that I should go out and find myself a proper job and get a mortgage?'

'Since when have I ever nagged you?' said Mum.

It was true, Mum never did nag Sebastian about

getting a proper job. Gran and Grandad thought it was disgraceful, the way he lived; Mum always spoke up for him.

'You'd better just hang on here till the cottage is free again.'

'But Maggie, it could be weeks.'

'So? If we've put up with you this long I guess we can put up with you a bit longer.'

'If you were still here at Christmas,' said Sophie, 'you could come to Parents Day and pretend to be my father!'

At the beginning of term, taking advantage of having Sebastian there, Martha went to Mrs Kincaid to ask if he could come into the school and give a talk to Year 10 on anti-vivisection and show the BUAV* video, *Health with Humanity*.

'Yes, I see no reason why not,' said Mrs Kincaid.

'After all, we had that farmer who came in last year,' urged Martha, 'trying to tell us how fox hunting was a good thing.'

'And you gave him a pretty rough ride, as I recall?'

Mrs Kincaid's eyes sparkled behind her glasses. Martha sometimes had the feeling that Mrs Kincaid was more sympathetic to the cause of animal rights than she let on. She supposed, being a head mistress, she felt she had to be impartial. 'You'd better try and arrange it for a lunch hour or after school. I don't want members of staff complaining that their teaching time is being eaten into.'

Martha had just gone to all the trouble of fixing up for Sebastian to come in at 3.30 the following Tuesday, and had written out notices to put on the various notice boards around the school, when she was called into the office and informed by Miss Tyrell that 'I'm afraid you're going to have to cancel it,

* British Union for the Abolition of Vivisection.

Martha. There's been a complaint from the Science Department.'

'Miss *Widlake*!' said Martha. It had to be.

'She feels it's wrong to present only one side of the argument. Too much like propaganda.'

'She didn't say that when we had the farmer!'

'No, well – ' Miss Tyrell spread her hands. 'I'm sorry. That's the message.'

'She could always come along,' said Martha, 'and put her side.' If she dared. Sebastian would soon demolish her. 'She could even get someone from the Research Defence Society. They could show their rotten video, as well.' She had no fear of the RDS. She had seen their video, and it was pathetic. Sebastian would wipe the floor with them.

'I'll try putting it to her, if you like,' said Miss Tyrell, 'but I don't hold out much hope. She sounded pretty adamant.'

The answer came back, and the answer was no. Miss Widlake did not personally have the time to waste engaging in what she called 'futile argument' and she didn't think the spectacle of the RDS and Sebastian trying to score points off each other would be either edifying or instructive.

'I think what she's really scared of,' confessed Miss Tyrell, 'is that a lot of you girls will be too easily swayed by emotional arguments. It makes it very difficult for Miss Widlake, afterwards, when she has to teach you.'

'But we don't use emotional arguments!' said Martha. 'We use scientific ones!'

'Look, I'm not the person you have to convince. Go and have a word with Miss Widlake. See if you can persuade her.'

She couldn't, of course. Miss Widlake hated animal rights people with as deep a hatred as the animal rights people hated the vivisectors.

'I would remind you, Martha,' she said, tight-lipped, 'that before I became a teacher I used to be a research chemist . . . *I do know what I'm talking about*. I will not tolerate anyone coming into this school, interfering in *my* subject, indoctrinating *my* pupils, with a load of pseudo-scientific sentimental eyewash!'

'It's not eyewash!' Martha said it angrily. She knew she was asking for trouble, but why should Miss Widlake be allowed to get away with it just because she was a teacher? She stood there telling the most appalling untruths, blackening the entire animal rights movement, and Martha was expected to say nothing? Just listen in meek silence? Sebastian wouldn't! (Neither would Sophie.)

'Did you know,' said Martha, 'that there's an organization in this country called Doctors against Animal Experiments? *Doctors*,' said Martha. 'You can't accuse them of being pseudo-scientific and sentimental!'

'They have obviously not checked their facts,' said Miss Widlake. 'They have not worked in the field: I have.'

Martha was taken aback. 'You mean you've actually tortured animals? You've actually injected them with lethal doses? You've actually given them cancer? You've – '

Miss Widlake cut her short.

'That,' she said, 'is the very reason I will not have animal rights people coming into this school! You are demonstrating exactly the kind of brainwashed hysteria that I wish to avoid. If you can't discuss the subject rationally, then it's best not to discuss it at all.'

'You call it brainwashed,' shrieked Martha, 'to care about the way people treat animals? You – '

'Martha Randall,' said Miss Widlake, 'I am giving you due warning! I can take so much and no more.

There comes a point when I snap. That point has now been reached. Go away and cool off. You may come back later and apologize.'

'Apologize for what?' muttered Martha.

She managed just in time to stop herself crashing the door shut behind her. Even as it was she would probably be put on report. For a moment she quailed: if there was one thing Mrs Kincaid would not tolerate it was impertinence to members of staff. Girls had been suspended before now. Mum would go mad if she were suspended.

Well, and so what? Sebastian had actually gone to prison for his beliefs. He hadn't flinched. Neither would Martha.

That evening, in the secrecy of her bedroom (just in case Mum should see and start asking questions), Martha took a felt tip pen, one of the ones with a thick point, and wrote out a series of notices on pages torn from a drawing block. There was one notice which said, *DANGER! SUPPRESSION OF FREE SPEECH*, another which said, *DID YOU KNOW YOU ARE BEING DEPRIVED OF YOUR BASIC RIGHTS?*, another which said, *NAZI GERMANY IS ALIVE AND WELL AND LIVING IN THIS SCHOOL!* All the notices, in smaller letters at the foot, bore the message: *Meeting outside school gates, 3.30 today*.

The following morning, armed with Blu-Tak and drawing pins, she marched determinedly about the school pinning up her notices in prominent places where they couldn't possibly be missed, such as over the mirrors in the senior cloakroom, inside the door of the games cupboard, on the trunk of the chestnut tree at the entrance to the playing field. By break time, the whole of Year 10 was agog.

'Who is it?'

'Who's doing it?'

'What's it about?'

'Someone's going to catch it,' said Ros, as she and Martha took their usual after-lunch stroll round the playing field.

'Why?' said Martha. 'It's a free country.'

'Yes, but come on!' Ros nodded towards the chestnut tree, where Martha had stuck her Nazi Germany notice. 'That's political.'

'Everything's political,' said Martha. Sebastian had taught her that. Everything, in the end, came back to politics.

'There's politics and politics,' said Ros. 'Mrs Kincaid'll go mad if she sees that. She wouldn't mind if they said *democracy* was alive and well – '

'But that's the whole point!' said Martha. 'It isn't!'

Ros looked at her, askance.

'It wasn't you,' she said, 'was it?'

'Not telling! You'll have to wait till 3.30!'

'Martha Randall, you are stark staring barmy,' said Ros.

At 3.30, Martha took up her position outside the school gates. A fair-sized crowd had already gathered. Martha felt a bit trembly, but buoyed up with a sense of the rightness of what she was doing. It was appalling that free speech should be suppressed – and in a school, of all places! In any case, she was *outside* the school gates, not in, so they couldn't accuse her of trespassing or misusing school property. If a person wanted to voice a person's mind on the public highway, then a person had every right to do so. At least, as far as Martha was concerned.

Martha put her school bag on the ground and stood on it. She set her hands, trumpetlike, to her lips.

'I am here,' bawled Martha, above the hubbub and roar of passing traffic, 'to alert you to a very serious fact. Namely, that *freedom of speech*, one of our *basic rights*, is being *denied* to us *here in this school*. And why is it being denied to us? Because certain elements amongst those who call themselves our *teachers*, who are supposedly here to *enlighten* us, are terrified of our hearing *any other point of view save their own*. This,' bellowed Martha, 'is where totalitarianism starts and democracy ends! This is how it all began in Nazi Germany! This – '

A snigger interrupted her.

'You can laugh!' yelled Martha. 'You won't think it so funny when the thought police arrive and start hammering on your door in the middle of the night! You w–'

'Martha Randall,' hissed an irate voice from somewhere behind her, 'stop that this instant!'

Martha swung round.

'I'm exercising my right to free speech!'

'Yes, and bringing disgrace upon the school! Get along home, the lot of you!' Miss Widlake made furious shooshing motions with her hands. 'You ought to be ashamed of yourselves! Behaving like a rabble!'

'There's no law – ' began Martha.

'On the contrary,' snapped Miss Widlake. 'There are several laws. 1. You are obstructing the highway 2. You are causing a public nuisance 3. You are being libellous.'

'I didn't say anything that wasn't true! And we're not obstructing the highway, there's loads of room for people to get past. I w–'

'Right! You have now gone too far.' Miss Widlake breathed deeply, flaring her nostrils as she did so. 'I'm sorry, but you leave me no option.'

Martha stood for a moment, uncertain, as Miss Widlake turned and strode back, on thin beanstalky legs, into school. Was she supposed to wait for her, or what? She knew a moment of unease, but dismissed it as unworthy. Sebastian had had to put up with far worse than this.

'What do you reckon?' said Ros, who had lingered

when the rest of the crowd had dispersed. 'Gone off to fetch the thumbscrew and the rack?'

'Probably gone to put me on report.'

'Well, you are a bit of a nutter,' said Ros. 'You do ask for it.'

Martha picked up her bag and slung it defiantly over her shoulder. 'I'm only sticking up for our rights.'

More importantly, she was sticking up for animals' rights. Animals had no voice of their own: it was up to people like Martha to speak for them. She felt that Sebastian would approve.

Sophie arrived home, wide-eyed, five minutes after Martha.

'Is it true?' squeaked Sophie. 'Did you really call Miss Widlake a Nazi?'

'Yes,' said Martha, 'but for heaven's sake don't tell Mum!'

Mum got to hear of it anyway. Two days later there was a letter from Mrs Kincaid, suggesting that a meeting between her and Mum might be a good idea, to 'solve some of Martha's behavioural problems'.

'Behavioural problems?' wailed Mum. 'What have you been up to now?'

'It's Miss Widlake,' said Martha. 'She won't let us show *Health with Humanity* because she says it's propaganda and we'd all be brainwashed. She won't even let us show it if the other side come and show theirs. I mean, that's suppression of free speech, isn't it?' She turned, appealing to Sebastian. 'All we ever get are *her* views. That's just as much propaganda as anything else. Did you know – ' Martha leaned forward to Sophie – 'she used to be a *vivisectionist*?'

'She looks like one,' said Sophie. 'All mean and pinched.'

'She said I'd got to apologize to her because I accused her of torturing animals.'

'I hope you didn't?'

69

'Yes, I did! I did accuse her!'

'No, I mean apologize.'

'No, I did not!'

Sophie giggled. 'You just called her a Nazi, instead!'

Sebastian choked on a mouthful of toast. Mum said, 'Martha, you are utterly wretched! Can't you ever learn discretion?'

'Why should she?' said Sophie.

'Because otherwise I get bombarded by notes from headmistresses asking me to come in to meetings that I would far rather not have to go to! *Honestly*.' Mum stuffed Mrs Kincaid's letter irritably down the side of her bag. 'As if I don't have enough to do!'

'Well, I'm sorry,' said Martha. 'But you can't just take these things lying down. Can you?'

She turned again to Sebastian.

'Don't ask him!' said Mum. 'He got turfed out of school for calling his headmaster a fascist thug.'

'Oh! *Sebastian*. Did you?'

'You never told us!' said Sophie.

'You never asked,' said Sebastian.

'In any case,' said Mum, 'I should hardly think it's the sort of thing one would be proud of.'

Martha wasn't so sure about that. She wouldn't ever call Mrs Kincaid a fascist thug, because Mrs Kincaid wasn't. But Miss Widlake. . . .

'Just put it right out of your head,' said Sebastian.

That evening, after school, Mum had her interview with Mrs Kincaid.

'We'd better not start supper till she gets in,' said Sebastian, and when Sophie, impudent, said 'Why not?' and reached out a hand to start picking, Sebastian retorted, 'Because it's bad manners, that's why not!' and slapped her wrist for her. Just like a real father, thought Martha. Sophie stared at him, reproachfully.

'I'm hungry!' she said.

'Too bad! You'll have to wait.'

'Mum's having to wait,' said Martha.

'That's because of you, that is! Not me!'

'I was fighting the cause. We're all in it together. Just shut up and do what Sebastian tells you.'

'For once in your life,' added Sebastian.

Mum arrived back at last. She wasn't looking cross, Martha was relieved to note, but on the other hand she wasn't exactly looking pleased, either.

'We waited supper for you,' said Sophie, taking all the credit.

'Pour me a large cup of tea,' said Mum, 'I need it. I have had a very trying time . . . Miss Widlake was there. She is a very trying woman. *Nevertheless* – ' Mum raised her voice, warningly, as Martha tried to cut in – 'I have some sympathy with her.'

'Mum!'

'You let your passions carry you away,' said Mum. 'No one minds you putting forward your views – '

'Miss Widlake does!'

' – it's the manner in which you put them forward that people are objecting to.'

'But she was suppressing free speech!'

'You get all the free speech you need in the High Street every Saturday.'

'That's not the point! It's not the point! Is it?' Martha pleaded with Sebastian across the table. 'Free speech ought to start in school!'

'It ought,' agreed Sebastian. 'Unfortunately, it rarely does.'

'So one ought to fight for it! It's a basic right – and it's for the animals. They *need* us. If we let people like Miss Widlake get away with it, spreading all her lies, then– '

'Oh, Martha, for God's sake just be quiet! I'm sick

71

of it! Day and night, it's all I ever hear! Your voice is becoming intolerable.'

'But, Mum, it's – '

Sebastian leaned across and tapped her on the back of the hand with the handle of his knife.

'Cool it! OK?'

'But, S–'

'I said, *cool it*!'

Martha subsided, albeit resentfully. She knew now how Sophie had felt: they weren't used to Sebastian being masterful.

They ate for a while in silence. Sebastian had just started a carefully neutral conversation on the subject of gardening – 'We could have a wych-hazel tree. Have you ever thought of having a wych-hazel tree?' – when there was a loud shriek of horror from Sophie, who had been ferreting in the fridge in search of more food.

'Who bought this?' She waved a vacuum-packed bag of vegeburgers.

Mum bristled. 'I did,' she said. 'Why?'

'We can't eat them! They've got whey in them!'

'So what?' said Mum.

'So it's not vegan!'

'Too bad! I haven't got the time to waste wading through long lists of contents just to satisfy your esoteric tastes!'

'But, Mum, it's easy! You don't have to! There are *dozens* of vegan vegeburgers. This one will have to be fed to the animals.'

'You give that back!' said Mum. '*I* shall eat them. I'm not vegan. And why is that dog picking at her food like that? What's the matter with her?'

'It's a new diet.' Sophie announced it, proudly. 'Veggiedog. We've got a whole great big sack of it . . . vegetarian food specially for dogs.'

'Oh, *Christ*!' said Mum.

'It's all right,' said Sophie, 'she's just got to get used to it. All the others have.'

'What about the cats? You're not trying to convert them, are you?'

Sophie shook her head. 'Cats are different. They need meat, they're carnivores. Dogs are like us: omnivores. They can eat anything. Though as a matter of fact,' said Sophie, 'I don't know whether you know it but I was reading in this book that human beings aren't really made for eating meat, our intestines are too long. All the meat hangs about and festers in them and that's why we get bowel cancer. True carnivores have very short guts so – '

'Spare me the lecture!' snapped Mum. 'I'm going to go and put my feet up and watch the television, and *I do not want to be disturbed*. Do I make myself plain? Have you got the message? Good!'

Mum snatched up Bigwig and left the kitchen, slamming the door behind her.

'Mum's in a mood,' said Sophie. She crouched down beside Becky, trying to coax her with handfuls of vegetarian dog food. 'She will get used to it, won't she? The Veggiedog?'

'She'll get used to it. Don't you worry about her. Cats will starve themselves to death sooner than eat something they don't fancy, but not dogs.'

'Is it quite fair?' said Martha, suddenly stricken. Poor Becky! She did so love her food.

'It's perfectly fair,' said Sebastian. 'She's too plump, anyway.'

Later in the evening, without telling anyone, Martha crept out to the kitchen and opened a tin of cat food for her.

Next week was Mum's birthday. Sebastian, in an effort to please – Mum had been a bit funny lately, ever since the Miss Widlake incident – was going to clean the house from top to bottom and prepare a special gourmet all-vegan meal, which the girls knew about but not Mum.

The day before, while Mum was at work, the postman called with a big important-looking parcel from Henley-in-Arden. Sebastian set it on the table for her to see when she arrived home.

'Heavens!' said Mum. 'What on earth have they sent me?'

Sophie pounced. 'You're not to look till tomorrow!'

'But I want to know what's in it!'

'*Childish*,' scolded Martha, though she was just as curious as Mum. Gran and Grandad never sent big parcels as a rule, they said it was a 'sheer waste of money', just pouring funds into the maw of the GPO.

Next morning at breakfast Mum was allowed to open her presents. Gran and Grandad's was a leather coat. There was a stunned silence as Mum drew it out of its folds of tissue paper. Sophie was the first to speak.

'Mum,' she said, 'that's *awful*!'

'Why have they done it?' whispered Martha. But she knew why they had done it: it was their way of showing contempt for Sebastian and everything he stood for. It was their gesture of defiance. A challenge to Mum: now let's see how strong your so-called principles are. . . .

Slowly Mum held the coat up against her. She slipped an arm into one of the sleeves. Sophie stared at her, aghast.

'You're not going to wear it? *Sebastian*! Don't let her!'

'Nothing to do with me,' said Sebastian, quietly.

'No, it isn't! Dead right!' Mum had the coat on now and was heading for the hall to look at herself in the long mirror. Sophie fled after her, her face screwed up in anguish.

'Mum! You can't! That's dead animal!'

'I didn't kill it,' said Mum. 'I didn't buy the coat. It's a present from my parents. Me not wearing it isn't going to bring the animal back to life, is it?'

'No, but, Mum – ' Martha said it earnestly, politely, trying to show sympathy but at the same time anxious that Mum should understand – 'it's a statement. A *political* statement. How can we be seen with a mother who wears leather? It's almost as bad as fur.'

'Nonsense!' said Mum, doing a little twirl in front of the mirror.

'It is! It is! Sebastian! Tell her!'

Sebastian was leaning against the kitchen doorway, watching as Mum pranced and pirouetted, showing off her dead animal skin. He shook his head. 'My lips are sealed.'

'They'd better be!' said Mum. 'And you, cat!' She flapped a hand at Bonny. 'Keep off! We'll have no claws on this coat!'

'Mum, you are a *traitor*!' yelled Sophie.

'Doesn't that make a nice change?' said Mum.

That evening when she came home – wearing the coat – Mum had bought herself a large cream bun, all horrible and squidgy, which she ate very slowly and deliberately in front of them to round off Sebastian's vegan meal.

'It's my birthday,' said Mum. She licked her lips, collecting up great gobbets of cream. 'I'm sick of perpetually being told what I can and cannot eat . . . I'm sick of *being lectured*.'

'You will get sick,' said Sophie, 'eating all that.'

'And fat,' said Martha.

'I don't care,' said Mum. 'Do you hear me? I *do not care*.'

75

Martha watched her a moment in silence. 'You're just being purposely defiant,' she said.

'Maybe I am,' said Mum. 'So what? I haven't taken the pledge.'

'I hope you feel guilty as *hell*!' screamed Sophie. 'That's a veal calf you're eating!'

'It's cream,' said Mum.

'Yes, and it was meant for calves, not for human beings. If it weren't for people like you stuffing themselves with their milk, all the little calves could have it and not be sent off to be made into veal! You're nothing but a murderer!'

'Hey! You!' Sebastian pointed sternly at Sophie across the table. 'Enough! This is no way to treat your mother on her birthday.'

'But what a way to celebrate!' said Sophie. 'Eating cream that's been stolen from tortured animals!'

Sophie was too young, thought Martha: she didn't realize why Mum was doing it. Martha wasn't altogether sure that she did, though she had a faint idea. She thought perhaps it was a bit like Ros going on and on about her latest favourite pop star, who at the moment was someone called Bo Jest, trying to make Martha see just how marvellous and wonderful and altogether brilliant he was and in point of fact having just the opposite effect, because all her gushing simply made Martha feel hostile, which was obviously what Mum was feeling.

It wasn't that Mum was out of sympathy, just that sometimes it all got a bit too much for her, living with three fanatics. Martha could understand that. She herself had turned on Ros only last week and ill-temperedly informed her that Bo Jest was a stupid sort of name for a stupid sort of person and that anyway his ears stuck out. Ros had been really hurt, just as Sophie was, now.

'Stop sulking,' said Sebastian. 'And stop preaching! That's no way to win people over.'

'You're a fine one to talk!' snapped Mum.

She was obviously feeling ratty with absolutely everybody.

Next morning when they came downstairs, something terrible had happened: Mum's new leather coat was hanging over the back of a chair, shredded into a thousand pieces.

'My coat!' cried Mum.

The cats, congregated on the draining board and the work surface, waiting for their breakfasts, purred loudly: they had done a good job.

'But how did it get there?' gasped Martha.

Everyone turned, to look at Sophie.

'*Sophie*!' said Mum. 'It was you, wasn't it? You gave it to them on purpose!'

Sophie sobbed, and admitted it. Even Martha was shocked. Sebastian picked up the shredded remains of the coat.

'Maggie, I'm really sorry about this,' he said.

'Why?' Mum turned on him, viciously. 'What's it to do with you? You didn't tell her to put it out for the cats, did you?'

Sebastian recoiled. 'No, of course I didn't.'

'So what are you apologizing for?'

'I sometimes get the feeling that in your heart of hearts you hold me responsible for Sophie's excesses.'

'Don't you talk to me about excesses! Your life has been nothing *but* excesses from the word go. And yes, I probably do hold you responsible! You're the one she gets these ideas from. You're her hero – you're the one she slavishly copies!'

'Maggie,' said Sebastian, 'please – '

'Oh, just leave me alone!' Mum snatched the ravaged remnants from him and headed for the door. 'I'm sick to death of the lot of you!'

'She shouldn't have *wanted* to wear it,' said Sophie, as she walked into school that morning with Martha. Sophie was chastened yet by no means repentant. 'She's been as hateful as can be, just lately!'

'How can you say that?' Martha looked at her, reproachfully. 'When she rescued Clancy for you? *And* Amelia.'

'They were my birthday and Christmas presents! And why is she always so mean to Sebastian? Picking on him all the time – as if it's his fault!'

'I think – ' Martha hesitated, trying to find the words to explain. 'I think sometimes she gets a bit fed up with always having to – to live up to him. To his standards. I think she'd like it better if he weren't quite so . . . single-minded.'

'But then he wouldn't be Sebastian!'

'No,' agreed Martha. Sebastian *wouldn't* be Sebastian if he didn't care so deeply.

'And she loves him,' said Sophie. A note of anxiety entered her voice. 'She does love him, doesn't she?'

'Yes, I'm sure she does or she'd have found someone else years ago and got married again. But I think maybe you can love someone and at the same time find them impossible.'

'Sebastian's not impossible! He's the nicest person I know! And he's a *good* person.'

'Christ was a good person,' said Martha, 'but I bet you couldn't have lived with him.'

Sophie regarded her, doubtfully.

'You'd better not let Miss Widlake hear you say that – ' Miss Widlake took them for RI as well as for science– 'or you'll be in even more trouble.'

'Think I care?' said Martha.

6

'Sebastian, darling Sebastian! You will come, won't you?'

Sophie wound her arms about Sebastian's neck and rubbed her cheek against his in what Martha personally considered a distinctly nauseating fashion. She had *never* behaved like that with Sebastian, even when she was young and syrupy.

'*Please*, Sebastian! Say that you will!'

'But it's for parents,' said Sebastian.

'That doesn't matter! If you haven't got any parents, anyone will do. There's a girl in my class whose parents are abroad, so her grandmother always comes.'

'Ah, that's different. That's because her grand-mother is in *loco parentis*.'

Sophie blinked. 'Pardon?'

'Standing in for her parents.'

'So you can stand in for my parents! Well, one of them.'

'What about Martha?' Sebastian, not without diffi-culty, screwed his head out of Sophie's embrace and twisted round to look at her. 'Doesn't she have any say?'

'It's nothing to do with her! This is lower school; she's upper. They had their parents day last term. You've got to come,' said Sophie, 'cause I've told everyone you are.'

'Have you asked Maggie?'

'Mum's coming anyway. She always comes.'

'No, I mean . . . have you asked about me coming? She might not want me to.'

'Why shouldn't she?'

'I might do something to upset her, or make her ashamed.'

'But *I* want you! I can pretend you're my dad.'

'Except that everyone knows he isn't.' Martha said it bluntly. It was about time Sophie grew out of these childish daydreams. It was really embarrassing, the way she carried on.

'Not everyone,' said Sophie. 'Some people'll think he is.'

'That could be awkward,' said Sebastian.

'It wouldn't! It would be lovely! I'm going to tell Mum you're coming.'

'You are going to *ask* her,' corrected Sebastian, 'whether I *may*.'

'Oh, all right!' Sophie crunched up her face. 'But I know she'll say yes.'

Considering that Sophie was still in disgrace over the shredding of the leather coat, Martha thought she had a pretty huge cheek asking Mum anything at all, but Mum had been in a bit of a better mood just lately. She hadn't even complained about the expense when Biscuit, the new cat, had got bitten by Bigwig and had had to go to the vet. In fact she had even made a fuss of him and told Bigwig to mend his manners. (Bigwig had simply puffed himself up and gone to sit with icy contempt on top of the television.) When Sophie, in the horrible winsome ickle-girly voice which she sometimes assumed, lisped out her request 'Mum, Sebastian *can* come to Parents Day with us, can't he?' Mum said yes, of course, if he wanted.

'So long as he doesn't disgrace me by yelling at

members of staff that they're wearing animal skin. Or fur. Or eating something he doesn't approve of. Or drinking cows' milk in their coffee. Or wearing make-up that isn't kosher. Or – '

'He wouldn't know,' said Sophie, 'would he? He wouldn't know what make-up they were wearing.'

'That wouldn't necessarily stop him,' said Mum.

'Well, but if he *promised* not to – '

'I promise on my honour,' said Sebastian, 'to be deaf and dumb and not say a word – if I'm still here, that is.'

'You've got to be here! Why shouldn't you be here?'

Sebastian glanced quickly at Mum. 'I can't sponge off you for ever,' he muttered.

'You do not *sponge*,' said Mum. 'You fill the girls' heads with impossible principles, you fill the house with animals and there are times when you irritate me beyond belief, but one thing you do not do is *sponge*. And you've got to be here next weekend whether you like it or not.'

'Why?' said Martha. 'What's happening next weekend?'

'I'm taking time off to go to a conference. Sebastian is going to stay here and play daddy.'

'Oooooh! Daddy!' Sophie squealed and launched herself at him. 'Will you tuck us up in bed and tell us bedtime stories?'

Sophie really could be utterly *sickening* at times.

Mum went off straight after work on Friday. On Friday evening there was a telephone call for Sebastian from one of his AFF friends asking for urgent reinforcements for a circus picket on Sunday afternoon. The circus in question was an old enemy – Turtle's Travelling Circus, complete with elephants and tiger, a roller-skating polar bear and sea lions that jumped through hoops.

'Where are they performing?' said Martha. 'Not locally? I thought Bromley had banned circuses with animals?'

'They've managed to find a farmer who's rented them a field.'

'*Farmers*!' Martha said it with contempt. 'Trust a farmer! I bet it was the one who came and told us about fox hunting.'

'So what time are we going?' said Sophie.

'I'm not sure that you're going at all. Martha can come if she likes; that's OK. But – '

'Why her?'

'Because I'm older than you,' said Martha.

'What's that got to do with it?'

'Circus pickets have a habit of getting out of hand. I don't think Maggie would be too pleased if I took you along.'

Sophie's face turned slowly scarlet. Martha could see her preparing to dig her heels in. No one was more obstinate than Sophie when she really put her mind to it.

'If I can't go, then neither can she! Mum wouldn't like me to be left here on my own.'

'At twelve?' said Martha. 'Can't be left on your own for just one afternoon?'

'If I'm old enough to be left on my own I'm old enough to come to a circus picket!'

'What do you reckon?' Sebastian turned, for guidance, to Martha. 'Do you reckon Maggie would mind?'

'Of course she wouldn't!'

'I don't see why she should. Really.'

'She lets me go leafletting – she lets me go on the march!'

'Yes, and sometimes the march is quite hairy.'

'Well, if you're sure,' said Sebastian. 'If you're not just saying it – '

'She isn't just saying it! It's true! I'm not a *child*.'

'In that case, you'd better not behave like one. I don't want any trouble. Just stick with me and do what I tell you. No breaking ranks. OK?'

Sophie nodded, solemnly.

On Saturday morning, because there was no leafletting, they went into Bromley to have what Sebastian called 'a blitz' on circus posters. Whenever they saw one which had been stuck up illegally – on the windows of empty shops, on doorways, on advertising hoardings on top of other people's ads – they either tore them down or if they couldn't do that then they scribbled over them with the same black pen that Martha had used for her Nazi notices. Sebastian had explained that to take the posters down was perfectly legal, so long as they remembered that officially the posters were the property of the circus and by rights had to be handed back to them. It probably wasn't legal to scribble over them, but then it wasn't legal for the circus to stick them up in the first place. At one point, as they were ripping down a poster from an empty shop front, an elderly woman came up to them and asked them what they were doing.

Sebastian said politely, 'We are removing circus posters, madam.'

'Yes, I can see that,' said the woman. 'What I wanted to know was what you were doing it for?'

By way of reply, Sebastian held up the poster which they had just torn down. On the front was a photograph of a polar bear, muzzled, standing on its hind legs with its feet strapped into roller skates.

'That,' said Sebastian, 'is what we're doing it for.'

The woman fished in her bag for a pair of glasses. She put them on.

'Quite right, too,' she said, after she had studied the poster. 'The best of luck to you!'

'If only everyone were like that,' sighed Martha.

'If everyone were like that,' said Sebastian, 'there wouldn't be any bears on roller skates in the first place.'

Next afternoon, before they set out on the picket, he asked Martha once again if she were sure it was all right for Sophie to be with them.

'You know your mum's feelings on things like this better than I do. She won't let you go hunt sabbing, will she?'

'No, but that's because she's scared we'll get trampled on, or horsewhipped. This is just like leafletting, really, isn't it? I mean, all we're going to do is give out leaflets, right? She won't mind that.'

'Well, just make sure,' said Sebastian, 'that you stay with me.'

Martha had never been on a circus picket before. She, Sophie and Sebastian were posted at the entrance to the field to catch people on their way in for the evening performance, while a bunch of AFF supporters stood at the exit to hand leaflets to those coming out of the matinée.

'This is all we're here for,' said Sebastian. 'Just to give out leaflets. Whatever you do, don't get drawn into any acrimonious exchanges with circus people.'

Sophie and Sebastian stood at one side of the entrance, Martha at the other. Most of the people coming in took a leaflet, though one or two shook their heads and hurried past, and just occasionally someone would shout provocative remarks at them, but they were used to that from their Saturday morning sessions in Bromley.

Martha, who had been on anti-vivisection pickets outside laboratories, was even used to people such as lab assistants and doctors shouting abuse at them.

What she wasn't used to was actual physical abuse. She was really shocked when a short, swarthy, tousle-haired man wearing jodhpurs and carrying a riding crop walked over from the Big Top and deliberately spat at them. And in spite of priding herself on having read *Lady Chatterley's Lover* and *Viz* magazine and knowing all about four-letter words, she was equally shocked by some of the insults that followed. She began to wonder, rather nervously, whether Sebastian had been right about not bringing Sophie – not that Sophie was exhibiting any signs of distress. On the contrary, she was showing a dangerous propensity for shouting back. Sebastian was having to put his hand over her mouth to stop her. He had *told* her not to get involved.

'You keep animals locked up in cages!' shrieked Sophie, breaking free of Sebastian's restraining hand. 'You k–'

Sebastian's hand silenced her again, but too late: the damage had been done. The horrid little gnome in jodhpurs, lips drawn back in a grin of triumph, roared towards Sophie brandishing his whip. Martha screamed, as the whip came down – but it was Sebastian who caught it, not Sophie. As he thrust Sophie to one side, the whip went lashing across his face. Sophie, like an idiot – she was brave, but she was *stupid* – lunged forward, yelling. Just in time, Sebastian managed to catch her by the arm and yank her back. The gnome stood, legs straddled, a grin splitting his face from ear to ear.

'Have you up for trespassing,' he said.

Martha realized what he had done: with carefully calculated insults, he had drawn Sebastian – thanks *entirely* to Sophie disobeying orders – on to circus property. He may have struck the first blow, but Sebastian was now equally in the wrong. Sophie was

85

an *idiot*. She was too young; she was a liability. She didn't know how to restrain herself.

There were no more people coming in to the circus. The gnome had picked his moment well: the lane was empty of all save animal rights workers, while on his side of the gate, suddenly, from seemingly nowhere, another half dozen of his colleagues had sprung up. Even Sophie needed no persuading that the moment had come to make their exit.

They walked back in a bunch down the lane. Sebastian's face was bruised and bleeding; the sleeve of Sophie's anorak had been half ripped out.

'Are circus pickets always like that?' said Martha, shaken.

'Only – ' Sebastian mopped at his face with his handkerchief – 'when people who ought to know better do what they were specifically told not to do and engage in acrimonious discussion.'

'It wasn't even a discussion,' said Martha. 'It was a slanging match.'

'Yes, she rose to the bait magnificently . . . it's the oldest trick in the book. Taunt someone long enough and you'll goad them into replying.'

'Sorry,' said Sophie, in a small voice. She seemed for once to be genuinely contrite.

'Don't worry,' said Sebastian. 'You'll learn.'

Mum arrived home at nine o'clock that evening. The first thing to meet her eye as she came through the door was Sophie's anorak hanging in the hall with its one arm trailing floorwards like a broken limb: the second was Sebastian's face. He had an angry red welt running from the corner of his left eye down to his chin.

'What on earth,' said Mum, 'have you been up to?'

There was silence; then Sophie, mumbling rather, said, 'We went on a circus picket.'

'You did what?'

'Went on a circus picket.'

They had discussed whether or not they ought to tell her. Sophie and Martha had both been for keeping it from her – 'She'll only get in a flap. We could always say we were playing with the dogs, or something' – but Sebastian had insisted.

'I can't lie to Maggie. I only ever lied to her once. I'm not doing it again.'

Martha had known it was a mistake: she had known Mum would blow up.

'Went on a *circus* picket? Not Turtle's?'

Sebastian dropped his gaze. 'Yes, I'm afraid so. I'm sorry, I shouldn't have taken them.'

'Damn right you shouldn't have taken them!' Mum whirled round, angrily, on Martha. 'Are you aware someone got badly injured on a Turtle's picket last month? Ended up in hospital with a punctured lung? These circus people don't just stand idly by, you know! They fight back – it's their livelihood that's at stake. And if you weren't aware of it – ' she swung back to Sebastian – 'he certainly was!'

'Yes, I know,' said Sebastian. 'I'm sorry.'

'Stop saying you're sorry all the time! What does it mean, *sorry*? When you keep doing the same things over and over and – '

'Mum, it was an emergency!' said Martha. 'They needed people in a hurry. It wasn't Sebastian's fault. He asked me. I was the one who said you wouldn't mind.'

'He shouldn't have had to ask you! He knows perfectly well that I'd mind. God, I can't even go away for forty-eight hours but you get yourselves into trouble!'

'It wasn't *much* trouble,' said Sophie. 'Just a man with a riding crop, running at us. And yelling things. Were you frightened?' she said to Martha. 'I wasn't. I knew he wouldn't really do anything.'

'What do you mean, wouldn't do anything? How did Sebastian's face get into that state? And what happened to your anorak?'

'Oh. That,' said Sophie. 'I think it got caught on something. And Sebastian sort of . . . walked into a bush. Wasn't looking where he was going.'

'No! Too busy rescuing you from maniacs with riding crops.'

'I didn't need rescuing! I – '

'Sophie,' said Sebastian. He put a finger to his lips. 'You want me to come to your Parents Day, don't you? Well, then . . . stum!'

It was a pity the circus picket had turned nasty. Mum had been in a really good mood before then; now she was back again in the sulks. Well, not exactly sulks, but showing a definite tendency to be *picky*. She bawled at Buster for digging a hole in the lawn, which was something which wouldn't normally have bothered her, the lawn being mainly a collection of clover and plantain. She had a go at the cats because one of them had sicked up a fur ball on the bathroom floor – (what did it matter? In the *bath*room?) – and cursed Clancy and Amelia for getting out of their field and trampling on the garden. Martha could have understood it had it been a proper garden, with flower beds and herbaceous borders, but all it was was shrubs and fruit trees. When Sophie admitted that it had probably been her fault for not shutting the gate properly, Mum snapped that that was 'no more than she had come to expect from this ruddy rotten family.' The ruddy rotten family exchanged glances and prudently kept quiet.

'Anyone would think,' grumbled Sophie, afterwards, 'that she was going through the menopause.'

88

'I don't think that happens till you're about fifty,' said Martha. 'Does it?' She prodded at Sebastian.

'Does what?' Sebastian, with an air of deep abstraction, was washing the dishes.

'The menopause,' said Martha. 'It doesn't start till you're about fifty.'

'Or does it?' said Sophie. 'Is Mum having it?'

'No, of course she isn't! What are you talking about?'

'Her being so ratty all the time. She went on and *on* about me leaving that gate open.'

'Serve you right! People that leave gates open deserve to be gone on and on at. Suppose it had been a gate into a road?'

'Well, it wasn't,' said Sophie, 'was it?'

'The principle remains the same ... *don't do it again.*'

Heavens! thought Martha. Now they were both ratty.

Two weeks later, at half term, Martha went off with Sebastian to do a picket at a research lab. This time, playing safe, she asked Mum's permission first.

'Where is it?' said Mum.

'Not far. Someone's going to give us a lift from Croydon.'

'You mean you're going to pollute the atmosphere?'

'Yes, because we want to get there for eight o'clock so we can hand out leaflets as people go in to work.'

'So what is this place, exactly?'

'It's horrible. They not only experiment on animals they breed them, as well, and send them abroad for vivisection. Like those beagles that time that got suffocated.'

'That place was closed.'

'Yes, that's what we want to do with this one . . . force them to shut down.'

'Force them how?' said Mum.

'Well, by picketing. Leafletting. Getting people to sign petitions, writing to the papers, writing – '

'So long as there's not going to be any violence,' said Mum.

'*Violence?* They're the people who use violence! Not us.'

'All right, so you just make sure that you don't. I don't want any trouble.'

Martha and Sebastian had to leave home at half-past five in the morning. Sophie, who had been grizzling and whining for the past week because she wasn't allowed to go with them, and who had sworn she was going to wake up at five-thirty and accompany them whether they liked it or not, predictably remained fast asleep in her bed. If there was one thing Sophie was bad at, it was getting up in the morning. Martha wasn't quite sure why Sebastian had refused to let her go, since research workers, unlike circus people, were *on the surface* quite civilized – i.e. they might torture animals but they didn't generally run at you with riding crops or knock you down in their cars – but Sebastian was adamant: Sophie was not coming and that was that.

Martha didn't argue the matter. Sebastian could be quite stern when he wanted and in any case it made her feel pleasantly important, going off with him by herself. Even so, she remained puzzled. He wasn't one for featherbedding, and Sophie had been on lab pickets before. Maybe, she thought, it was because it was an AFF gig, and he knew how Mum felt about the AFF. She was the first to admit that they did some good work – infiltrating labs and taking photographs of the atrocities that went on – but she didn't like it when they burned meat lorries or planted fire bombs in fur shops. Most of all she didn't like it when they, or at any rate Sebastian, got put in prison.

When Martha and Sebastian arrived home, late in the evening, they found Mum watching television and Sophie all puffed up with her own exploits: Sophie had been out and about pushing Veggie Pledge leaflets through people's doors.

'I pushed one through a *church*, and I gave one to a *butcher's*, and I – '

'Quiet!' said Mum. 'I want to hear what the others have been up to.'

'Just picketing,' said Sebastian.

'All day?'

'We went leafletting round the town, then went back for the afternoon shift. We didn't get away till gone six.'

'And it's taken you all this time to get back?'

'We came by bus. Several buses.'

'All the way from Godalming,' said Martha. 'We're g–'

'Godalming?' Mum froze. She looked across at Sebastian. 'Where in Godalming?'

'NORLABS,' said Martha. 'We're going to g–'

'NORLABS?' said Mum. 'You took her to NOR-LABS?'

'Why not?' said Martha. She glanced from Sebastian back to Mum. What was the problem now? 'We're going to go there again, aren't we? We're going to keep the pressure up until they're forced to give in. And if they *don't* give in – '

'What?' said Sophie.

'Some more direct sort of action may have to be taken.'

'Like what?'

'Like maybe they might get broken into.'

Mum and Sebastian were still looking at each other:

steadily, gaze for gaze. It was almost as if Mum were issuing some kind of challenge.

'They've got to be stopped,' said Martha. 'One way or another.'

Mum breathed, deeply. Martha turned eagerly towards her.

'It's like in the war, when they had concentration camps . . . you'd have approved of people breaking into concentration camps and rescuing the prisoners, wouldn't you? So why not animals? I don't see there's any difference. Suffering is suffering,' said Martha. 'And if the law won't help then you just have to take the law into your own hands. You can't just sit by while animals are tortured and do nothing, just because the law says it's all right for them to be tortured. Bad laws,' said Martha, growing desperate in the face of Mum and Sebastian's continuing silence, 'are there to be broken. It's your *duty* to break them. If you care enough. It's the only way to get things done. Just sitting around talking isn't going to do it. People talk and talk and – '

Quite suddenly, Mum stood up and left the room.

'What's her problem?' said Sophie.

'Stay there.' Sebastian peeled himself off the sofa and went after her. Sophie and Martha exchanged glances.

'In one of her moods,' hissed Sophie.

But she hadn't been! thought Martha. She had been quite happy. She had wanted to hear what they had been doing. What had happened to make her go all strange and quiet? Sophie turned back to the television.

'It was you, talking about breaking the law.'

'I didn't mean *I* was going to.' Small chance of Sebastian ever letting her do anything exciting. Martha scrambled to her feet and went out into the hall. From the kitchen, came the sound of Mum's

92

voice. Martha hesitated a moment, then crept on
tiptoe down the passage, followed by two of the cats.
She could hear Mum quite clearly.

'You promised me! You gave your word! You'd
never get the girls involved in anything!'

'Maggie, I haven't! I wouldn't. I – '

'Taking her to that place! That place of all places!
You think I don't know what – '

'What's going on?' whispered Sophie.

'Sh!'

'Are they having a row?'

Sophie, unashamedly, pressed her ear to the door
crack. Martha hovered nearby. She heard her mum's
voice – 'I trusted you!' – and guilt overcame her. She
beckoned urgently at Sophie.

'Come away!'

Sophie shook her head.

'Well, I'm going!'

Martha shot off, up the stairs, all five dogs galloping
behind her. A few minutes later, Sophie appeared.
She flung herself down on Martha's bed.

'Mum's *shouting* at him.'

'I don't want to know,' said Martha. 'It's mean to
eavesdrop.'

'But she's being really horrid to him – and he's just
standing there, taking it.'

'So what do you expect him to do? Beat her up?'

'I wouldn't stand there and let her yell at me,' said
Sophie. 'If she said to me some of the things she's
saying to Sebastian – '

Martha snatched up a pillow and folded it down
over her ears. 'I don't want to know!'

'But she's being really unkind. She – '

'Sophie, will you just *shut up*!'

Later, when Sophie had been persuaded to go to
her own room, taking three of the dogs with her,
Martha crept back downstairs for a drink of water.

Mum and Sebastian were still in the kitchen. This time she couldn't help hearing.

'I know you didn't plant the bloody bomb! You've already told me! But you've only got yourselves to thank if they blame you for it. You're the ones that have spawned all this violence – it's being done in your name!'

'Oh, now, Maggie, come on!' Sebastian's voice, unlike Mum's, was gentle and reasonable. Mum was screaming like a banshee. 'That's like saying religion is to blame for all the blood that's been spilled in the name of Christ. Or Mohammed. Or Moses.'

'Well, it probably is! And don't you talk to me about religion, you – you renegade! Bloody atheist preaching to me about religion!'

'All I'm trying to do – '

'All you're trying to do is make excuses! Well, I've had it with you and your excuses! *Maggie, I'm sorry, Maggie, I didn't mean it, Maggie* . . . I've listened to them for twenty bloody years! I've just about had enough!'

Martha turned and bolted back to her bedroom. People who eavesdropped never heard anything nice.

Next morning when they gathered in the kitchen for their cups of peppermint tea before taking the dogs out, Sebastian wasn't there. Mum, looking pale and tired as if she hadn't slept, simply said that he 'had gone'.

'And please don't become hysterical, Sophie. I'm not in the mood for it this morning.'

'But when is he coming back?'

'I don't know when he's coming back.'

'But what about Parents Day? He'll be back for Parents Day?'

'I have no idea. Most probably not.'

'But he promised!'

'You ought to have learnt by now,' said Mum,

'that Sebastian is not always in a position to keep his promises.'

'Mum! That's not fair!' The tears started into Martha's eyes. She couldn't bear the thought of Sebastian – Sebastian, who had never harmed anyone, whose only crime was to care passionately about all the suffering in the world – being turned out of the house with nowhere to go. 'Just because he took me on a picket!'

'It wasn't just because he took you on a picket, it was where he took you on a picket. And all this talk of direct action . . . *I do not want you involved.*'

'I wasn't involved! I won't be involved! He'd never let me! He always says, Maggie wouldn't like it!'

'Well, he's right, I wouldn't, and I've had enough! I'm not sure that I want him coming here again.'

'*Mum!*'

'Yes, and you can stop looking at me like that! I know you both think Sebastian's some kind of a saint and I'm a nagging harridan, and maybe in some ways he is a kind of saint, but believe you me saints aren't always the easiest of people to have relationships with. I think it's high time you two girls had your eyes open about a few things. Just wait there!'

Mum flew out of the kitchen. They heard her footsteps thudding up the stairs – it sounded as if she were going all the way up to the attics. Sophie and Martha sat looking at each other without speaking. Even Sophie, for once, appeared to have nothing to say. The calamity which had overtaken them was too big for mere words. Sebastian! thought Martha. Oh! Sebastian! She knew now how it felt to have a heart that was breaking. How could they live without Sebastian?

'There!' Mum flung a book on the table between them. 'Take that away and have a read and maybe you'll understand a little better. Until then, I should

95

be grateful if we could just get on with our lives as before. Sophie, pass my tea, would you, please – and *get that cat off the table!*'

7

They waited till Mum had left for work then scuttled off with their trophy, and all five of the dogs, to sit in the summerhouse at the bottom of the garden. (Sebastian had built the summerhouse as a birthday present for Mum, three years ago.)

'What is it?'

Sophie peered eagerly over Martha's shoulder. The book which Mum had tossed at them was long and thin with stiff red covers. On the front a label had been stuck, bearing the words **STRICTLY PRIVATE & CONFIDENTIAL. HANDS OFF!!! That means YOU**.

Martha opened it at the first page. There, in large looping writing which she could just recognize as Mum's, she read:

Sat. May 13, 1972. Now that I am starting a new life, I am going to keep a journal so that I can look back on it in years to come and marvel at how young and naive I used to be.

'What's it say?' Sophie craned forward. 'What is it?'

'I think it's Mum's diary.'

'Diary?' Sophie snatched at it, greedily. Martha held it, for a moment, at arm's length.

'It doesn't seem right to read someone's diary.'

'But she wants us to read it! That's what she gave it to us for.'

97

'Yes, I know, but – ' Martha wasn't sure that she wanted to be let into all Mum's youthful secrets. Whatever Sophie said, it seemed like prying.

'Let's have a look.' Sophie grabbed and began reading out loud. '1972 . . . how old was Mum then?'

Martha humped a shoulder.

'If she was thirty-nine last birthday – '

'Eighteen,' said Martha. She was better at maths than Sophie was.

'"Now that I am starting a new life" – that wasn't when she got married, was it?'

'No, of course it wasn't! She didn't get married at eighteen.'

'People do,' said Sophie.

'Yes, well, Mum didn't. If we're going to read it – ' Martha tugged the book back towards her – 'let's have it where we can both see it.'

Strictly speaking, continued the journal, *I suppose I ought to begin by going into all the details of my life thus far, but that is just plain boring. All I shall say is, THIS IS THE JOURNAL OF ME, MARGARET EASTER: HER JOURNAL.*

Easter had been Mum's maiden name. Her best friend at school had been called Valerie Flowers, so that in the register they had always appeared as Easter Flowers. Martha remembered Mum telling her that.

I am only going to record matters of interest. Some days, if nothing particular happens, I shan't bother to record anything at all. Today, however, something particular did happen: I moved out of Station Road –

'What was Station Road?' said Sophie.

'I'm not sure. I think it's where she had her bedsitter.'

'Where she met Sebastian?'

'Yes; while she was doing her business studies

98

course. And then she gave that up and went to medical school.'

'I wonder why she gave it up?'

'Came to her senses, I should think.' Business studies seemed to Martha an ignoble thing to do.

'So when she says she's starting a new life,' said Sophie, 'does that mean she's starting at medical school?'

'Not in the middle of May. Look, just read it and shut up!'

– *I moved out of Station Road,* wrote Mum in her journal, *and came up to London to live with Aunt Lizzie.*

Martha remembered Aunt Lizzie. She had been Gran's elder sister, so that in fact she had been Martha's Great-Aunt. She had been fun – unlike Gran – but unfortunately she had died when Martha was quite young. Sophie probably didn't remember her at all.

Mum wanted me to go and live in Chislehurst with Dot, continued the journal. *She thinks Aunt Lizzie is fast and rackety. This is because Aunt Lizzie is a theatrical agent and Mum is terrified I shall meet Undesirable People, meaning actors and actresses and people who smoke pot. Would that I could!!! Fortunately my hours at the bookshop –*

'What bookshop?'

'*I* don't know!'

– *make Chislehurst not possible. I have to be there by eight-thirty every morning, and there is just no way I could manage to wake up early enough to be in London by that time.*

(I say fortunately because I think it would drive me mad to live with Dot. She is obsessed by babies. Sebastian also likes babies but is not obsessed by them, thank goodness. Dot keeps muttering about us both going to visit him and taking the baby with

us as she is convinced this would make him better overnight. I think it would be more to the point to take Sunday. Sebastian loved that cat so much, but I'm not sure hospitals will let people take animals in.)

'*Hospital?*' said Sophie.

'Shut up,' said Martha. 'Just read!'

I am starting at the bookshop tomorrow. I'm not sure whether I'm looking forward to it or not. It's only a stop gap until I can start at medical school – if I get accepted!!! – but I suppose it might be interesting. If there aren't any customers I can always sit down and read Gray's Anatomy.

Sun. May 15 – Dot and I went to visit Sebastian. He is much better than he was but is having to take drugs to stop him being depressed.

'*Sebastian?*' said Sophie.

Martha pulled an irritated face. Couldn't Sophie read in silence?

Jesse says maybe he will always have to take drugs, though perhaps not all of the time, just when he starts getting low. Jesse says he is probably a manic-depressive, meaning sometimes he is very excitable and up in the air and sometimes he is suicidally depressed. Dot disagrees with this. The good thing about Dot is that she really likes Sebastian (because of him being good with the baby, I suspect and also not being thuglike, like Chris).

'Uncle Chris!' Sophie crowed, delightedly. 'He's still thuglike!'

Dot says the only thing wrong with Sebastian is that he cares about things too much and takes everything too much to heart, all the time thinking about animals and the terrible things we do to them, not to mention the bomb and pollution and nuclear reactors. Jesse said, 'That way madness lies.' I agree that you have to shut off a part of your mind and just pretend certain things aren't happening, even though you know that they are. You can't afford to dwell on them, which is what Sebastian does. He dwells. And his parents don't help. They don't even try to understand him. They just think he's wet and loopy and a pain. I know he can be tiresome –

'Oh, *poor* Sebastian!' cried Sophie. 'Why is everybody always against him?'

'Mum wasn't, from the sound of things.'

'But she is now. She –'

'Look, just *read*, will you?'

I know he can be tiresome because even I have yelled at him, like the time he went racing into a butcher's shop and started to rant and rave and harangue people, it was just so embarrassing, but still I would far rather have someone like Sebastian, who cares too much, than someone like Chris, who doesn't care at all. What would be perfect would be someone who cares as much as Sebastian but is a bit more stable, I was going to say like Jesse, but although Jesse is nice he does't really care about things the way Sebastian cares. Jesse, for instance, still thinks that experiments on animals are necessary. He says that he doesn't like them, but if they help human beings there is no alternative. Sebastian disagrees violently with this, and I think so do I though I get a bit muddled about it at times. It's something I must discuss with Sebastian when he's well enough to be faced with dismal reality. I don't want to do it now in case it plunges him back into depression. He thinks he will be able to go back to Oxford next term. I do hope so.'

The next few entries were all about Mum working at the bookshop; then there was a gap of several weeks, when presumably nothing of interest had occurred, then a long detailed account of a theatrical party that Aunt Lizzie had taken her to.

'I don't want to read about this!' said Sophie. 'I only want to read about Sebastian.'

They flipped through the next few pages, skim-reading until Sebastian's name cropped up.

22 June – Went with Dot to visit Sebastian again. Took him a tape of Schubert's quintet because he once told me it was sublime and one of his favourite pieces of music. (I tried it and can't get on with it. Just sounds like a noise.)

'She listens to that sort of stuff all the time now!' said Sophie.

'Obviously Sebastian's influence.'

29 June – Went to see Sebastian without Dot but took Sunday with me in her cat-carrying basket. I asked last time if I could and they said yes. Sebastian was really chuffed, I knew he would be. But he said it's best if Dot keeps her because although he's leaving hospital next week he's got to go and live at home until he goes back up to Oxford, it's one of the conditions of letting him go. He said his parents aren't very good with animals, in spite of being farmers – or do I mean because of being farmers? He says they're always killing things – foxes, crows, pigeons. Rabbits. Mice. He says their motto is, if it moves, shoot it. Except for the cows, of course: they're milked dry and then sent to the slaughterhouse.

'You see, she *does* know better,' said Sophie.

I think it's ridiculous sending Sebastian back home. He'll just be upset the whole time. He can't bear to see animals being killed. I wish he could come and stay with me and Aunt Lizzie, but I don't see any way. She's only got one spare room, and I'm in that. I don't expect she'd let us sleep together because of what Mum would say (though I don't think Aunt Lizzie would mind for herself, being used to Immoral Theatricals) but in any case I haven't yet decided whether I want to. I mean, sleep with Sebastian or not. No, I don't, I mean have sex with Sebastian. (I hate saying 'sleep with': it's so coy.) If I were going to do it with anyone it would be with him; but do I want to do it with anyone?

Sometimes I think one thing, sometimes I think another. Dot in her Dottish way says that 'these things happen in their own good time' and that I shouldn't let myself feel pressurized. I don't feel pressurized, but when Sebastian said goodbye to me today he kissed me – properly, not just a peck – so that I'm pretty sure he would like to. Have sex, that is.

'Hah!' said Sophie.

'Belt up,' said Martha.

30 June – I have been thinking about having sex with Sebastian. I wonder what it would be like? I don't think I'm scared of it, just worried in case I mightn't enjoy it, or worse still in case I actually might hate it, and then where would that leave us? It's funny that in spite of being in many ways a very spiritual sort of person – caring about cruelty, listening to classical music, reading poetry, etc. – Sebastian is just the same as all other boys (men? He's nearly nineteen) when it comes to this one particular thing.

'You wouldn't think she'd want us reading all this,' said Martha, 'would you?'

'I think it's nice,' said Sophie, turning over the page. 'I like hearing about her and Sebastian when they were young.'

Between the end of June and the beginning of September there was a gap: obviously not much had happened in Mum's life during that period. The journal started again on September 15th, but Sebastian wasn't mentioned for several entries.

'There,' said Sophie, pointing.

23 Septr – Sebastian came to stay for the weekend before going back to Oxford. (And before me starting at medical school. I am feeling nervous!!!) Aunt Lizzie said, 'I'm sorry if I sound old-fashioned but it's going to have to be the sofa for your young man . . . your mother would never forgive me if I encouraged Natural Goings-On to go on.'

You can tell that Aunt Lizzie really thinks Mum's attitude is pretty puerile. I do, too, but at least it saved an embarrassing situation since Aunt Lizzie obviously thinks that we already indulge in natural goings-on and I would have found it difficult to explain that we didn't. She might think me strait-laced, moving as she does in theatrical circles.

24 Septr – We did it! We actually finally did it!

'Did what?' said Sophie.

Aunt Lizzie went off to see a show that one of her clients is in and we stayed indoors by ourselves and it just sort of happened. Quite naturally. By which I mean that it seemed right. And inevitable. And I didn't hate it!

'Oh, *that*,' said Sophie.

It wasn't quite what I had expected, but then I'm not really quite sure what I had expected. It was nicest afterwards, when we just lay there and cuddled.

'You've gone all red,' said Sophie, looking at Martha.

Sebastian said he hoped it hadn't been too bad, and I said it hadn't been bad at all, only a bit peculiar – it is *peculiar, when you stop and think about the mechanics of it, which as a medical student I suppose it is natural that I should do. Sebastian assures me it will be 'loads better next time'. How does he know??? And who says there's going to be a next time?*

26 Septr – Sebastian was right: it is loads better the second time round!

'I hope they used condoms,' said Sophie, all prim and proper. 'She never even *mentions* AIDS.'

'AIDS wasn't around then. People could carry on just as much as they liked.'

'Goodness!' said Sophie. 'They must have been at it all the time.'

'They were. Whenever you read books that were written in those days they did nothing *but* jump into bed together.'

'I can't imagine Mum, can you?'

Martha thought about it.

'I can imagine Mum. I can't imagine Sebastian.' (Or perhaps it embarrassed her too much.)

'Oh, I can imagine *Sebastian*,' said Sophie.

They skipped the next few entries, about Mum starting at medical school – 'We can always go back and read that later' – and moved on to the middle of October.

21 Octr – Sebastian came for the weekend. I think Aunt Lizzie must have noticed a change in our relationship because first she asked us if we'd like to go to a party with her, and then she said, 'No, I suppose on second thoughts you'd rather stay here and have the place to yourselves.' I said that we would, because of Sebastian not being good at parties – he says that too many people all at once confuse him and make kaleidoscopes in his brain – but I could tell she didn't believe me, even though in fact it happens to be true.

3 Novr – Sebastian has gone vegan! (Gone loopy, Aunt Lizzie says.) This means he doesn't eat any animal produce at all – no eggs, cheese, butter or milk. It also means he doesn't wear any leather or even wool. Or of course fur. He says he's sent every-thing that was non-vegan to be sold for animal charity. This means that he is left with hardly any clothes. Also, as far as I can see, there is not very much he can eat, other than vegetables. He turned up with his own personal carton of soya milk and his own tub of marge. When Aunt Lizzie pointed out that she already had marge he said yes, but hers wasn't any good because it had whey in it, and whey was a milk product. Oh, and he also said that he has become an Animal Freedom Fighter, or what he calls 'an AFF activist'. According to Sebastian, anyone can be an AFF activist simply by carrying out AFF-type actions, e.g. breaking into research labs, damaging butchers' shops, etc.

Aunt Lizzie said it all sounded rather alarming, and I agree, but Sebastian says it is the only way. He says that peaceful campaigning is all very well but that direct action is needed if anyone is ever going to sit up and take notice. He says that if you believe passionately enough in a cause then you ought to be prepared to go to prison for it, and if it means break-ing the law then that is what he will do.

I sometimes wish he wasn't quite so extreme. Another thing he has done is throw away the drugs that he was given to stop him becoming depressed. He says they have all been tested on animals. I tried arguing with him. I said that even if they had it wasn't his fault and if it's the only way he can stop being depressed he ought to take them, but he said he'd rather be depressed than ride on the backs of tortured animals. He said that would depress him even more, and he doesn't believe in drugs anyway.

I am beginning to wonder whether I want to go in for psychiatry after all. I was only going to do it so I could help people like Sebastian, but if he won't take drugs what is the point?

'I didn't know Sebastian *ever* took drugs,' said Sophie.

'Sometimes you can't help it,' said Martha.

'Well, he doesn't now! And he doesn't get depressed.'

'He does occasionally. When he stops to think too much.'

'Oh well,' said Sophie, 'anyone'd get depressed if they thought too much.'

Sophie wouldn't, thought Martha. Sophie was irrepressible.

9 Novr – Sebastian is going to come and spend Christmas with us. I asked Aunt Lizzie and she said, 'By all means, if that is what you want. But won't your mother be expecting you in Birmingham?'

I told her about last Christmas, when Sebastian came up to Brum with me and how Chris had been so foul to him, telling everyone how he'd been a complete pain even when he was at school, and how Mum and Dad had no patience with what they called cranks, meaning, amongst other things, people who are vegetarians.

Aunt Lizzie agreed that Mum and Dad weren't the most tolerant of people. She was only scared that they might think she was coercing me if I didn't turn up. She said maybe I should go home for Christmas and Sebastian could come for the New Year? I thought about this, but then I thought, where would Sebastian go if he didn't come to us? He would have to stay in digs in Oxford all by himself and that would be horrible for him. Aunt Lizzie wanted to know, what about Sebastian's parents? and I had to explain about Sebastian's parents being even more unsympathetic than mine, what with his mother riding to hounds and killing foxes and his father being a hard-nosed farmer. Aunt Lizzie said, 'Oh, dear! Poor Sebastian! It's not really his scene, is it? In that case, I'll say no more. Let him come here.'

'I like Aunt Lizzie,' said Sophie.

'Yes, she was nice,' said Martha. 'I remember her, just a little.'

18 Novr – Went on a demo with Sebastian. Met some of his friends from the AFF. Not sure how I feel about them. I know they are all dedicated to the cause of animal rights but some of them seem very full of anger and suppressed violence. When I asked Sebastian about this he said that a) a sense of one's own helplessness in the face of suffering tended to make one angry (if it didn't make one depressed) b) that his colleagues in the AFF were not necessarily his friends: one had to work with all types and c) that he himself was too soft and was going to have to 'toughen up'. I am not sure what he means by this – he muttered something about 'not being so squeamish' – and I am not sure that I like it. I don't want Sebastian to toughen up! It's because he's gentle that I like him. I hate macho men who swagger and posture. On the other hand, if he could grow a second skin and not become so cast down I suppose it would be a good thing.

20 Novr – Aunt Lizzie asked me over supper this evening 'how involved I was' with Sebastian. She said, 'I don't mean physically, I'm not trying to discover whether you're sleeping together, but mentally. How committed are you?'

I thought about this for a long time. It seems incredible that I have only known Sebastian for just over a year and yet I feel closer to him than I have ever felt to anyone. In the end I said that I was totally committed without actually being in love, if being in love meant seeing people through rose-coloured spectacles, which I certainly don't see Sebastian through. I don't, for instance, go weak-kneed at the sight of him and I don't pine in his absence, but all the same he is the person who means most to me in this world.

I thought Aunt Lizzie looked a bit worried at this. I said, 'Why, anyway?' and she sighed and said that while she was extremely fond of Sebastian – she called him 'a lovely fellow' – he was none the less a man with a mission, haunted by all the cruelties inflicted by his fellow men, and she feared that if I threw in my lot with him there would be nothing but heartache.

'Why?' said Sophie, indignantly.

'You know why. We talked about it before. Crusaders,' said Martha, 'are not easy to live with. You, for instance, would be totally impossible.'

Sophie smiled: she liked that.

24 Novr – Went up to Oxford to spend the weekend with Sebastian as his room mate is away. Sebastian's digs are really grotty – one large room and a tiny sliver of kitchen right up at the top of a crumbling Victorian semi. It was nice to be on our own but all the time we were making love I kept thinking about what Aunt Lizzie had said about heartache. Sebastian asked me afterwards what the problem was. I said, 'I'm scared that I'll go and fall in love with you and life will be nothing but heartache.' He didn't ask me why I thought it would be heartache, or how I thought it would be heartache. All he said, very seriously, was 'Do you want us to stop doing it?' As if it's just the physical thing! Men are very stupid. Even Sebastian.

14 Decr – Sebastian rang to say he wouldn't be down this weekend as he has some demo or other that he has to go on. I asked if he would like me to come up to Oxford and go on the demo with him but he said it was not my sort of thing. What does he mean by this? What is 'my sort of thing'? I said, 'You're not going to go and smash windows or throw bricks, are you?' He said no, it wasn't anything like that, it was a big demo up in Manchester against a *drugs manufacturer. I don't know why he thinks that is not my sort of thing (maybe because I am studying medicine?) but anyway I can't really afford to go all the way to Manchester so that is that.*

It will be fun having Sebastian here at Christmas. I am looking forward to it.

15 Decr – Someone from college is actually driving up to Manchester tomorrow morning! (As a matter of fact it's Geoff Randall, who according to Tanya Burridge is 'interested' in me. I cannot imagine why as I am not at all a raving beauty and he is quite handsome.)

'Not as handsome as Sebastian!' said Sophie.

'Sebastian isn't handsome.' Honesty compelled Martha to admit it. 'He's nice-looking, but he's not handsome.'

'Well, who wants someone who's handsome, anyway?' said Sophie. 'All men that are handsome are drorgs.'

Whatever drorgs were. Sophie was always coming out with these weird expressions.

Geoff has offered me a lift if I want it but I've got to let him know by midnight as he's leaving at six. I've been trying to telephone Sebastian all evening only I can't get any reply. What a nuisance he is!

16 Decr – I rang Sebastian at one minute to midnight and there was still no reply. I bet he's staying overnight with a mate in Manchester. Why couldn't he have told me? Now I'm going to be stuck down here by myself. Perhaps I might go to Chislehurst to see Dot, though she'll only start nagging at me about not going home for Christmas. On the news it said that some big pot industrialist type had been kidnapped and his thirteen-year-old niece who was staying with him had also been taken. Aunt Lizzie said, 'How awful! Just before Christmas.' I suppose that would make it worse, if you were only thirteen years old. I used to adore Christmas when I was that age. We used to play games and dress up, even Mum and Dad. Now all they do is slump in front of the television. Christmas is not what it used to be. But it should be fun with Sebastian staying here. Aunt Lizzie is going to throw a theatrical party and we shall meet S*T*A*R*S . . . well, minor ones, anyway.

17 Decr – I am worried. It said on the news this morning that the people who kidnapped the industrialist and his niece are a group calling themselves the Animal Freedom Fighters. Aunt Lizzie said, 'Isn't that Sebastian's mob?' I said yes, but Sebastian was up in Manchester. Now I'm beginning to wonder. I've rung him and rung him and I still can't get any reply. I'm really scared.

In Aunt Lizzie's paper there is a picture of the girl who has been kidnapped. Her name is Penelope Monnery. There are also some dreadful pictures of animals that have been experimented on in NORLABS – '

'NORLABS!' Sophie jabbed a finger. Martha nodded.

– which is a place the industrialist is head of. It says in the paper that the AFF originally wanted Norman Monnery (he is the industrialist) to publish these pictures in his chain of newspapers that he owns and he wouldn't. I am not surprised. They are horrible. Like nightmares. And these are not the worst ones. They said they wouldn't publish the worst ones for fear of upsetting people too much. But these are quite upsetting enough.

I said to Aunt Lizzie that I could understand why the AFF had resorted to kidnap. Anyone that could do to animals the things that are shown in those photographs deserves whatever is coming to them.

'Good old Mum!' cried Sophie.

'She's not all bad,' said Martha.

Aunt Lizzie said she didn't think a court of law would see it quite in that light. She said they would take a dim view of kidnap no matter what the cause. She then said, 'Maggie, tell me honestly . . . you don't think Sebastian is mixed up in all this, do you?'

I just sat there and said nothing, but I could feel my cheeks glowing crimson. Aunt Lizzie said, 'All right, you don't have to answer if you don't want to. But you do know, don't you, that kidnapping is a very serious crime? And remember, there is a young girl being held. If anything should happen to her –'

No one knows why they took the girl. They seem to think that they weren't expecting her to be there.

'If anything should happen to her,' Aunt Lizzie said, 'public opinion will certainly not be on their side.'

I don't think I could bear it if Sebastian were involved in something like this! How long can you get for kidnapping? He could be shut away for life. Also it would mean that he had lied to me.

18 Decr – There is still no reply when I ring Sebastian's number. I tried telephoning his parents but his mother said, 'Sebastian? Why? Have you lost him again?' and gave one of her horrid tinkly laughs. She said that as far as she knew he was still in Oxford. Well, he's not – or if he is, he's not answering his phone.

19 Decr – Today I did something I don't think I have ever done in my life: I fainted. At six o'clock there was this knock on the door and I thought, 'Sebastian!' (Because we had arranged that he would come down this evening.) But it wasn't Sebastian, it was a policeman and a policewoman. They said could they come in and ask me a few questions. I was absolutely convinced they were going to ask me about Sebastian – whether I knew where he was, when I had last seen him, if he were a member of the AFF. I just conked straight out. One minute I was standing at the front door, the next I was crashing floorwards.

As it happens they hadn't come to ask about Sebastian, they had come because last week a girl was raped in this road and they wanted to know if we had seen anything (we hadn't). But after they'd gone, and I'd stopped fainting, Aunt Lizzie said, 'You thought they'd come about something different, didn't you?' She is so sharp, she doesn't miss a trick. It's probably because she's used to dealing with the-atricals and has had to learn when they're acting and when they're not.

She said, 'You thought they were going to ask you about Sebastian.' She told me that if I had any suspicions at all that Sebastian might be involved in the kidnapping it was my duty to go to the police. She said, 'I know it's not easy, when you love some-one, but think of that innocent young girl – think how her mother must be feeling. Think how you would feel if anything happened to her.' And then she said, 'Maggie, my dear, I am going to say some-thing which you may hate me for, but I have to say it . . . smashing bloke though Sebastian is, if you don't harden your heart now you will never be free of him.'

I know she is right, but how can I?'

'And why should she?' burst out Sophie, as Martha closed the book. (The journal, in spite of there being several unused pages, came to an end at that point.)

'I suppose – ' Martha said it gravely – 'I suppose Aunt Lizzie felt there wasn't much of a future in it.'

'But she loved him!' said Sophie. 'She says that she did! And he loved her! He still does!'

'So if he loved her, why did he tell her he was up in Manchester when he wasn't?'

'Cause maybe he was!'

'But if he wasn't – '

'It was a secret operation,' said Sophie. 'He couldn't go round telling just anyone.'

'Mum wasn't just anyone! He'd *made love* to her.'

'Yes, but – but he wouldn't want her involved,' said Sophie. 'Would he? Not if it was something dangerous. He was protecting her.'

'He wasn't protecting her: he was lying to her.'

'You don't know that! You're only saying it! You don't even know if it was Sebastian.'

Martha thought, it's obvious – or why else should Mum have stopped writing her diary?

'I'm going to ask her,' said Sophie. 'And if it *was* Sebastian, I don't blame him!'

That evening, when Mum arrived back from work, she said, 'Well? Did you have a good read?'

'Yes,' said Sophie, 'and we still think you should have married Sebastian instead of the other one.'

Mum faintly shrugged her shoulders as she sank down at the kitchen table. 'Tea?' she said.

'We've cooked you something,' said Martha, 'but it's not as good as Sebastian does.'

'I'll put up with it.'

'Mum!' Sophie bounced on to the chair next to her. '*Was* Sebastian mixed up in the kidnapping?'

'Yes. I'm afraid he was.'

'And did you go to the police like Aunt Lizzie said?'

'No. I'm afraid I didn't.'

'*Good*!' said Sophie. 'That man deserved to be kidnapped!'

Hastily Martha said, 'So what happened? Did they release him in the end?'

'Both him and the girl. In time for Christmas.'

'And was Sebastian ever – I mean – did they ever – '

114

'No.' Mum shook her head. 'He was never found out. He deserved to be, but he never was.'

'Why did he deserve to be?' Sophie sat up straight, prepared to do battle. 'Why do you say that?'

'Partly because kidnapping is a crime, partly because he was the one who was detailed to hold the girl. Apparently, the same day that he released her she actually saw his face. In other words, he wasn't a very good kidnapper. She could have led the police straight to him had she wanted.'

'But she didn't!' Sophie was jubilant. 'That's brilliant!'

'Is it?' said Mum. 'I suppose it is. He could have gone down for a very long time.'

'Did he tell you all this that Christmas?' said Martha.

'No. I – went home that Christmas, after all. Geoff – your father – rang me to ask if I wanted a lift, so – '

'I thought he was in Manchester?'

'He hadn't gone. It seemed as if . . . as if fate was telling me something.'

'You mean it was telling you to desert Sebastian!'

'Look, shut up,' said Martha. 'Sebastian was supposed to have turned up at Aunt Lizzie's, right? And he didn't, did he? And he hadn't even rung to let Mum know. *And* he'd lied to her. *And* worried her half out of her life, going round kidnapping people.'

'I was pretty mad at him,' said Mum.

'So when did he tell you about it? About the girl, and her seeing him?'

'Oh, that was years later. After your dad and I had split up.'

'Did you ever see Sebastian while you were living with Dad?'

'No. Your father didn't exactly encourage him. But at least,' said Mum, 'you can see why I was cross with him for taking you to NORLABS?'

'Y-yes. I suppose. But honestly he wouldn't ever have let me get involved in anything!'

'You will let him come back, won't you?' Sophie edged her chair closer to Mum's, cuddling up to her as she used to when she was little. 'You will, Mum, won't you?'

'I told him to stay away,' whispered Mum.

'But you didn't mean it?' persisted Sophie.

'I did at the time.'

'But not now?'

'I don't know!' cried Mum. 'Just stop bothering me!'

8

Life was very flat without Sebastian. They missed him when they came home from school. They missed him when they woke up in the morning. They missed him when they went for walks with the dogs. (Walks with Sebastian were always exciting: twice as long as normal and three times as adventurous. Mum complained they were like assault courses, but it hadn't ever stopped her coming on them.) They missed him for practical reasons – Sebastian's cooking was cordon bleu compared with Mum's – but mostly they missed him just for himself. He wasn't in the least a loud or noisy sort of person, yet the house felt horridly empty without him.

'There isn't anyone here when we get in!' wailed Sophie. 'We're latchkey kids!'

'Just like you were before,' said Mum. 'It didn't seem to bother you then.'

'That's because we didn't *know*,' said Sophie. 'We didn't realize how underprivileged we were. And it's not just us, it's the dogs! The dogs are all on their own. They shouldn't be! Dogs are social creatures. They'll get lonely.'

'All five of them?' said Mum.

'They'll pine,' said Sophie. 'They want Sebastian!'

It was Sophie who was pining. If she said it once a day, she said it a dozen times: 'It's just not the same without Sebastian.'

Sometimes Mum sighed, and sometimes she looked guilty, and sometimes she couldn't take it any more and snapped, 'Stop behaving like a spoiled brat! You got on perfectly well before!'

Before had been different: Sebastian had never stayed so long before. It had always been a quick overnight; a week or two at the very most. This time they had grown used to him being there, so that his absence left a gaping emptiness. Also, in the past, they had known that he would be back. Now Mum had sent him away and they might never see him again. It wasn't any wonder, thought Martha, that Sophie alternated between tears and fits of the sulks. Mum must know how much she loved Sebastian. Surely – it suddenly occurred to her – surely Mum couldn't be *jealous*? It wasn't that Sophie loved Sebastian more: only that she loved him as much.

Martha loved him, too, of course, but Martha was older and had her own ways of coping. She had a dream sequence that she lived through in her head every night before going to sleep.

In Martha's dream, she is at an animal rights demo all by herself – i.e. without either Mum or Sophie – when things turn nasty. She hasn't yet worked out who or what has caused the nastiness, whether it's pro-vivisectionists or hunt people or even the police, but suddenly everyone is in a panic and running for cover. And as Martha runs a voice calls out to her and it's Sebastian, and she's falling into his arms and he's holding her and kissing her and they're clinging to each other as if they're star-crossed lovers who've been torn asunder and at long last have come together again.

And in the dream they go back, hand in hand, to Sebastian's cottage in Northumberland where Sebastian makes love to her (except that she is not quite

118

sure what this would feel like and so she usually concentrates on her and Sebastian taking their clothes off and sliding into bed together and then lying in each other's arms after it has happened). She keeps trying not to think of Mum's journal, the bit where Mum says about her and Sebastian 'doing it', because this introduces Mum into the dream and tends to bring it back to earth, not to mention raising complications. She has yet to decide whether she has already left school and left home, and if so whether she is at university, and if so which one. She thinks perhaps Newcastle would be a good idea because then she could go to Sebastian's cottage and make love with him every weekend.

She doesn't feel guilty about taking Sebastian away from Mum because in her view Mum has forfeited all rights to him. In her waking moments she is aware that Mum has had a lot to put up with and that although Sebastian is a saint he is by no means blameless; but in her floating times, when she is almost asleep but not quite, she forgets any minor blemishes and elevates Sebastian to a state of near perfection. He is her dream lover, or how she imagines her dream lover: strong but tender, passionate but gentle, totally anti-violence yet at the same time fiercely protective (of Martha). He is her father figure and lover rolled into one.

Of course all this is the most horrible sentimental slush, like some dire TV soap. She is aware of it but none the less cannot help indulging. She doesn't only indulge in bed at night, either; sometimes she indulges in the daytime, when she ought to know better. It is like a drug. She has to try to ration herself otherwise there is a danger she will sink into a stupor and never come out of it. Needless to say, she has not confided any of this to Sophie. Sophie would think she had gone soft in the head. Or would she?

Martha gazed thoughtfully at Sophie across the tea table. It was there that most of the scenes of domestic upset between her and Mum seemed to take place. Sophie came in from school every day secretly hoping (Martha knew that she was secretly hoping even though Sophie hadn't actually told her) that Sebastian would be there. Every day she was disappointed – and every day she took it out on Mum.

'He was going to come to Parents Day!' sobbed Sophie. 'I've told everyone that he's coming!'

'Well, you shouldn't have,' said Mum. 'You know how erratic he is.'

'He wouldn't be erratic if you hadn't gone and s-sent him aw-way!'

Another day she accused Mum of 'just wanting to be rid of him', implying that Mum had found someone else. Mum got really mad at that. Martha couldn't decide whether she was mad because it was true or mad because it was untrue. If Mum had really found someone else then it would obviously make it a whole lot easier for Martha when she bumped into Sebastian at her animal rights demo and went off to make love with him in his cottage. But that was only dreams. In reality, she would feel every bit as devastated as Sophie if Mum took up with another man.

'Imagine,' said Sophie tearfully, one day, 'if he *died* . . . it would be all your fault!'

'Why would it be all my fault?' said Mum.

'And why should he die?' said Martha.

Sophie said he would die of neglect, having nowhere to live and no one to look after him. She said, 'You know you were always accusing him of not taking proper care of himself!' She then drew a soul-searing picture of Sebastian sleeping in a cardboard box with a little dog which he had rescued and both Sebastian and the dog freezing to death one cold winter's night 'just before Christmas'.

Mum said, 'Don't be so melodramatic! He's not that useless.'

'I didn't *say* he was useless,' said Sophie. 'He's like Mother Teresa . . . too busy caring about others to care about himself.'

'Oh, piffle!' said Mum.

That night Martha's dream takes a slightly different turn. In this version she is at college in London and on her way home one evening, after staying late at college (or maybe going to someone's party), she hears a whimpering sound and turns round to see this small bedraggled dog (it is of course the middle of winter, pouring with rain and freezing cold). The dog seems to want her to go with him, so she follows him and he leads her to this figure in a cardboard box. It is Sebastian . . . he is obviously ill, with a high temperature, though he recognizes Martha and feebly clasps her hand. Martha knows at once what she must do (no shilly-shallying: this is a dream, not real life). She runs into the road and hails a passing cab and rushes Sebastian (and the dog) back home to Mum, only because Mum is at work and Martha is now on vacation it is Martha who nurses him back to health, until one day he is feeling well enough to take her into his bed and make love to her, and there they are, living a life of sin under Mum's roof and having to keep it a secret both from her and from Sophie.

At various times, in the dream, both Mum and Sophie put their heads round the bedroom door at inconvenient moments, and in the dream this is very titillating and makes Martha go quite goose-pimply with excitement. It is an even more dreadful and soppy dream than her previous one.

Meanwhile, back in real life never a day passed but Sebastian's name was mentioned – almost always by

Sophie. She wondered aloud how he was, what he was doing, whether he had a proper bed to sleep in. One evening, on a note of triumph, she announced that Becky was eating her Veggiedog – 'Look!'

There was a silence. Mum was peeling potatoes at the sink, Martha preparing a nut roast for the oven, the radio burbling quietly to itself in the background.

'Eaten *all* of it,' said Sophie. 'What a good girl! What a good *good* girl! Look at that – ' she picked up Becky's plate and proudly showed it around. 'Sebastian said she'd get used to it. He was right. Sebastian's always right when it c–'

'Quiet!' Mum suddenly, without any warning, went ploughing across the kitchen and hurled herself at the radio. The voice of the newsreader came booming out at them:

' . . . now confirmed as the work of the Animal Freedom Fighters. The raid took place in the early hours of the morning. A night security guard was taken to hospital where he was treated for shock. He was later released. A spokesman for NORLABS – '

'NORLABS!'

'Sh!'

' – warned the public that the animals released in the raid would be quite unsuited as domestic pets. He said it was no kindness to take them out of the only environment they knew, and – '

'Crap!' said Martha.

'– he feared the trauma of their so-called liberation would only add to their suffering.'

'Can hardly be worse than being given cancer or ch–'

'Sh!' said Mum, but already the newsreader had moved on to other items.

'Wait for the headlines,' said Martha. 'They're bound to go through them again.'

They stood, the three of them, in suspended animation – Mum with a half-peeled potato in her hand, Martha clutching the nut roast, Sophie still waving Becky's empty bowl. The dogs, getting the message, sat bolt upright in a line, ears cocked, heads to one side. The cats lay around in heaps on the table, on the chairs, on the fridge, on the draining board.

'Now,' said Martha.

'Here are the news headlines once again. Last night's raid on NORLABS, in which fifty-two beagles and an unspecified number of cats and smaller animals were released, has now been confirmed as the work of the Animal Freedom Fighters. The Economic Community – '

Mum snapped the radio off. They weren't interested in the Economic Community; not at the moment.

'Sebastian!' crowed Sophie.

'They did it!' gloated Martha.

She and Sophie flung their arms round each other and performed a dance of jubilation round the kitchen, complete with nut roast, dog bowl and five dogs.

'They did it, they did it! They got into NORLABS!'

Round and round the kitchen danced Sophie and Martha. Buster, growing over-excited, jumped on the table, causing Bimbo to spring off in a fright and upset the milk jug. Ben, with one eye to the main chance, took a snatch at the nut roast as it passed. Beth and Becky started barking.

'This is madness!' cried Mum.

'But you must admit – ' Martha stopped, out of breath, tugging the nut loaf from between Ben's jaws – 'rescuing animals is a *good* thing to do.'

'Fifty-two!' exulted Sophie. 'I wonder where they've taken them?'

'Well, they can't all be sleeping in a cardboard box,' said Mum.

That night, Sophie rang Sebastian at his cottage in Northumberland, but the man who answered the phone was the man the cottage belonged to. He said Sebastian wasn't living there any more as he'd decided to take it over again himself. He had no idea where Sebastian was.

'There!' Sophie turned on Mum, reproachfully. 'I told you he wouldn't have anywhere to live!'

'And now we don't even know how to get in touch with him!' said Martha.

'He'll surface again,' muttered Mum, 'don't you worry . . . he's like a bad penny, that one.'

Next morning, when the paper was delivered, there was a picture of four masked men, dressed all in black, surrounded by beagles. The caption said, 'Members of the Animal Freedom Fighters with rescued beagles'. Even the press was talking of them being rescued rather than stolen. Sophie fetched Mum's magnifying glass and pored over the picture, trying to decide whether Sebastian was there.

'He is! He is! Look!' She handed the magnifying glass to Mum. 'The one at the back!'

Mum studied the picture long and closely.

'Well?' said Martha, impatient. 'Is it Sebastian?'

'I fear so,' said Mum.

Martha snatched at the magnifying glass. Why *fear*? Sebastian was a hero! People ought to get medals for doing things like that.

Mum, with a funny sort of laugh that sounded almost as if she might be going to burst into tears, said, 'Now, I suppose, he'll be turning up on the doorstep with half a dozen rescued beagles he wants us to take in!'

'We would, wouldn't we?' said Sophie. 'Mum, we would, wouldn't we?'

'No!' Mum seized the teapot and began angrily

sloshing tea into her cup. 'I've had enough! What does he think we are? An animal sanctuary?'

The atmosphere at school that day was quite different from the atmosphere on the day when the car bomb had gone off. Then, everyone had been hostile; now they were full of admiration.

'I wish they'd break into every single laboratory in the country and rescue *all* the animals!'

'It's hideous, what they do to them in those places.'

'Vivisection isn't any different from *murder*.'

Ros, who had seen the picture in the paper, whispered, 'Is one of them Sebastian?' Martha longed to be able to say 'Yes,' but she knew that she mustn't. If news leaked out, it could put Sebastian in danger.

'Can't tell who they are, can you,' she said, 'in masks?'

'I suppose not.' Ros said it regretfully. 'I suppose even if you could you wouldn't be able to say.'

'They could get done for it,' said Martha.

'The people who ought to get done for it,' said Ros, 'are the people who own the labs.'

'And the people who work in them.'

'*And* the people who work in them. I don't care if there is a recession, it's no excuse for torturing animals.'

The only person who struck a sour note was Miss Widlake, but Martha had expected that.

'I daresay,' said Miss Widlake, with a sneer, as she prepared to take 10B for physics, 'that you are all rejoicing at the so-called liberation of fifty-two beagles and countless numbers of assorted small mammals. I would remind you, however, that it needs only one, just one, of these "liberated" animals to be carrying some form of communicable disease for an epidemic to be started . . . in other words, this *daring act of rescue* –' her lip perceptibly curled as she said it – 'is in fact grossly irresponsible and could well put the whole community in the gravest danger. Far from applauding it, it cannot be too loudly condemned. You would do well to remember this and not let sentimentality overrule common sense.'

One or two of her favourites began niddy-nodding and turning censorious looks upon Martha, as if she personally had been responsible for the operation (she only wished that she had) but most people remained staunchly on the side of Sebastian and the AFF. As Ros said, tucking her arm companionably through Martha's as they walked round the field together during the lunch break, 'Miss Widlake is just as unbalanced as you are, but at least you are *nicely* unbalanced.'

Was it unbalanced, wondered Martha, to care so deeply about cruelty? Perhaps it just made you so.

That weekend they all, even Mum, expected Sebastian to arrive on the doorstep with his half a dozen beagles. Martha knew that Mum expected it because instead of slopping around all day in an old holey sweater and paint-spattered jeans she put on a brand new Animal Action sweatshirt and a pair of Lycra leggings which Martha had talked her into buying.

'You don't have to go all dowdy, just because you're middle-aged!'

Mum looked quite good in her sweatshirt and leggings. She had protested that she was too fat, and it was perfectly true that she was not sylph-like, but 'they make you look young and cuddly,' said Martha. She bet if Sebastian turned up now Mum wouldn't object to having a bit of a cuddle with him on the sofa. Martha wondered how she would feel if that were to happen and decided that on the whole she wouldn't mind too much. It would be worth it just to have Sebastian back again, and it needn't interfere with her daydreams. After all, it was in the nature of daydreams that you knew they wouldn't ever really come true.

Unfortunately it didn't happen because Sebastian didn't turn up. They waited till one o'clock on Saturday and midnight on Sunday, when Mum told Martha and Sophie rather sharply that it was 'Way past your bedtime. You'll never get up in the morning.'

Sophie didn't want to go to bed; she was still convinced that Sebastian would come. Next morning, when he hadn't, she burst into tears all over her cornflakes and sobbed that Mum had driven him away – 'He'll never come back now!'

'Just as well!' snapped Mum. 'He's a thoroughly bad influence!'

The end of term was coming up, and also Parents Day for the lower school. Sophie, swollen-eyed – she was doing a lot of crying these days – vehemently declared that Mum could go if she wanted but she would have to go on her own.

'I'm not coming if Sebastian's not here!'

Even Martha was starting to find that her daydreams no longer brought the solace that once they had. It was all very well fantasizing about Sebastian taking her back to his cottage, Sebastian kissing her, Sebastian making love to her, but when you woke up every day to the cold reality of his absence, daydreams, no matter how slushy and romantic, made a poor substitute.

Parents Day was on the Monday before they broke up. On Sunday evening Sophie retired to her bed, with three of the cats as hot water bottles, saying she had a stomach ache and felt sick.

'I don't know what to do about that girl,' said Mum.

Martha could have told her – 'Just ask Sebastian

to come back!' – but how could they ask him when they didn't know where he was?

'Are Sebastian's parents still alive?' she said.

'His mother is. Why?'

'I just wondered,' said Martha. Surely his mother would know? 'I just wondered where she lived.'

'She lives abroad. In Malta.'

'*Malta*?'

'There's nothing so terribly odd about it. A lot of rich retired people live in Malta.'

'Sebastian's never mentioned it.'

'They don't get on. She disowned him, years ago.'

'Oh.' So that was that; Sebastian's mother obviously wasn't any use. And Martha didn't know the names or addresses of any of the AFF supporters she had met. Members of the AFF tended not to hand out information like that.

'You'd think,' she said, 'the man who owns the c–' She stopped.

'You were saying?' said Mum.

'I was just trying to work out,' mumbled Martha, 'how we could get in touch with Sebastian if we needed to.'

'Wait till he gets himself arrested,' snapped Mum, 'then apply to HM Prison Service!'

That night, in Martha's dream, Sebastian is in prison and she is visiting him. She has just reached the part where Sebastian is about to make love to her when she falls asleep, which is probably just as well: it couldn't be much fun, making love in a prison cell.

Next morning, further along the passage, Mum's alarm clock had just started its horrible screeching, dispersing the last few lingering wisps of Martha's dreams, when from downstairs there came another sound, an abnormal one for that hour of the morning.

Martha stirred and stretched out her legs, carefully negotiating the two dogs that were under the duvet and the one that was on top. The alarm stopped: the other sound continued. It was the doorbell.

The doorbell!

Martha shot up the bed, scattering disgruntled dogs in all directions. Who would come ringing at the door at six o'clock on a Monday morning? Not the postman; he arrived punctually at half-past seven, as they came back from their walk with the dogs.

The ringing went on: two short, one long. Two short, one l—

Sebastian! It had to be Sebastian!

Martha catapulted out of bed, tripped over a dog, snatched up her dressing gown, stuffed her arms into it and stumbled out on to the landing in time to see Sophie, barefoot in her nightdress, throwing open the front door.

'*Sebastian!*'

It was! It was! Martha, forgetting to be shy, hurtled down the stairs pursued by barking dogs.

'*Shut those animals up!*' bawled Mum.

'Be quiet! Be quiet! *SHUT UP!*' roared Martha.

Mum came down the stairs in her old Marks and Sparks dressing gown covered in cat fur and muddy paw prints. Sebastian, still standing on the door step, pushed a lock of hair out of his eyes.

'It's all right,' he said. 'I know you don't want me to stay. I won't even come in if you don't want me to. It's just that I remembered it was Sophie's Parents Day, and I promised I'd be there. I didn't want to let her down – collar and tie, look!' He pointed. 'Nice school like that . . . won't let me in if I'm dressed all scruffy.'

Sophie gave a great screech. It sounded like 'Yeee haaaaa!'

'I thought you felt sick and had a stomach ache?' said Mum.

'That was last night! I've recovered now!'

'Amazing,' said Mum. She gestured, rather awkwardly, at Sebastian. 'You'd better come in,' she said.

'I won't if you'd rather I didn't. I can always meet you at the school.'

'Oh, don't be so ludicrous!' said Mum. 'We're just about to have a cup of tea and take the dogs out.'

'I could make the tea for you,' said Sebastian, 'if you like.'

'That sounds like a good idea,' said Mum.

'What about the beagles?' said Martha.

'Beagles?' Sebastian looked suitably blank. 'What beagles?'

'*You* know!' cried Sophie.

'We thought you'd bring us one to adopt,' said Martha.

'Would you like one?'

'No!' said Mum.

'Yes!' chorused Martha and Sophie.

'I could get you one if you want.'

'We do not want!'

'Mum we do! We do!'

'They're in desperate need of good homes. It's not easy finding the right sort of people, the poor creatures aren't used to affection. They need a lot of love – and of course they can't be advertised.'

'We do *not want a beagle*,' said Mum.

'Oh, Mum!'

'Think what they've been through!'

'Just one – '

'One little beagle – '

'Please, Mum! Let's just have one!'

'We could take one of the older ones – '

'One little darling dog saved from a fate worse than death – '

130

'Now, wait a minute! Wait a minute! Not so fast! You can't go adopting an animal that's been traumatized and leave it on its own all day. Who's going to look after it? Who's going to give it all the love and affection it needs?'

'Sebastian!'

There was a pause.

'You'll come and look after it,' wheedled Sophie, 'won't you?'

Sebastian glanced at Mum and quickly glanced away again.

'Well, someone will have to,' snapped Mum. 'I'm not taking the responsibility for it. I don't *want* any more dogs. And don't just stand there on the door step!' She grabbed Sebastian by the arm and yanked him through into the hall. 'Go and make that cup of tea and let's get out for a walk!'

Crossly, Mum stumped off up the stairs to put on her dog-walking gear. Sophie, in her nightdress, flitted after her.

'Mum, think of another name beginning with B! If it's a boy, we could call him Bertie. If it's a girl –'

Sebastian looked across at Martha.

'What do you think she wants me to do?' he said. 'Really?'

It was a temptation just to giggle and say, 'Make her a cup of tea!' That would be the easy way out. But Sebastian was asking her seriously.

Martha remembered what Aunt Lizzie had said – 'If you don't harden your heart now, you will never be free of him.'

Mum had tried to harden her heart, but at the last minute she hadn't been able to. That could only mean that deep down she didn't want to be free of him.

'I think,' said Martha, 'that she would like you to stay.'

131

He studied her. 'You're not just saying that? You really believe it?'

She was almost sure of it; as sure as you could be on someone else's behalf. If Sebastian were ever to be found lying sick in his cardboard box it would be Mum who looked after him, not Martha, for all her daydreams. Mum had always looked after him, she saw that now – defending him against her parents, against the hostility of the world. But Mum needed Sebastian just as much as he needed her.

'Martha?' Sebastian held out his hand. 'Tell me the truth! You do really believe it?'

'I do,' said Martha. 'Honestly!'

At that moment, Mum called out from the top landing.

'Is that kettle on yet?'

'No, ma'am! Right away, ma'am!' Sebastian tugged at his forelock. He pulled a face at Martha. 'At least I can make cups of tea, even if it's the only thing I'm any good at.'

Martha blushed.

'I don't expect it's the only thing,' she said.

Other great reads ╲ *from* **Red Fox**

BESTSELLING FICTION FROM RED FOX

☐ The Story of Doctor Dolittle	Hugh Lofting	£3.99
☐ Amazon Adventure	Willard Price	£3.99
☐ Swallows and Amazons	Arthur Ransome	£3.99
☐ The Wolves of Willoughby Chase	Joan Aiken	£2.99
☐ Steps up the Chimney	William Corlett	£2.99
☐ The Snow-Walker's Son	Catherine Fisher	£2.99
☐ Redwall	Brian Jacques	£3.99
☐ Guilty!	Ruth Thomas	£2.99

PRICES AND OTHER DETAILS ARE LIABLE TO CHANGE

ARROW BOOKS, BOOKSERVICE BY POST, PO BOX 29, DOUGLAS, ISLE OF MAN, BRITISH ISLES

NAME ....

ADDRESS ....

....

....

Please enclose a cheque or postal order made out to B.S.B.P. Ltd. for the amount due and allow the following for postage and packing:

U.K. CUSTOMERS: Please allow 75p per book to a maximum of £7.50

B.F.P.O. & EIRE: Please allow 75p per book to a maximum of £7.50

OVERSEAS CUSTOMERS: Please allow £1.00 per book.

While every effort is made to keep prices low it is sometimes necessary to increase cover prices at short notice. Arrow Books reserve the right to show new retail prices on covers which may differ from those previously advertised in the text or elsewhere.

BESTSELLING FICTION FROM RED FOX

☐	Blood	Alan Durant	£3.50
☐	Tina Come Home	Paul Geraghty	£3.50
☐	Del-Del	Victor Kelleher	£3.50
☐	Paul Loves Amy Loves Christo	Josephine Poole	£3.50
☐	If It Weren't for Sebastian	Jean Ure	£3.50
☐	You'll Never Guess the End	Barbara Wersba	£3.50
☐	The Pigman	Paul Zindel	£3.50

PRICES AND OTHER DETAILS ARE LIABLE TO CHANGE

ARROW BOOKS, BOOKSERVICE BY POST, PO BOX 29,
DOUGLAS, ISLE OF MAN, BRITISH ISLES

NAME...

ADDRESS...

....

....

Please enclose a cheque or postal order made out to B.S.B.P. Ltd. for
the amount due and allow the following for postage and packing:

U.K. CUSTOMERS: Please allow 75p per book to a maximum of
£7.50

B.F.P.O. & EIRE: Please allow 75p per book to a maximum of £7.50

OVERSEAS CUSTOMERS: Please allow £1.00 per book.

While every effort is made to keep prices low it is sometimes necessary
to increase cover prices at short notice. Arrow Books reserve the right
to show new retail prices on covers which may differ from those
previously advertised in the text or elsewhere.

Other great reads from **Red Fox**

Top teenage fiction from Red Fox

PLAY NIMROD FOR HIM Jean Ure

Christopher and Nick are each other's only friend. Isolated from the rest of the crowd, they live in their own world of writing and music. Enter lively, popular Sal who tempts Christopher away from Nick . . .
ISBN 0 09 985300 0 £2.99

HAMLET, BANANAS AND ALL THAT JAZZ
Alan Durant

Bert, Jim and their mates vow to live dangerously – just as Nietzsche said. So starts a post-GCSEs summer of girls, parties, jazz, drink, fags . . . and tragedy.
ISBN 0 09 997540 8 £3.50

ENOUGH IS TOO MUCH ALREADY
Jan Mark

Maurice, Nina and Nazzer are all re-sitting their O levels but prefer to spend their time musing over hilarious previous encounters with strangers, hamsters, wild parties and Japanese radishes . . .
ISBN 0 09 985310 8 £2.99

BAD PENNY Allan Frewin Jones

Christmas doesn't look good for Penny this year. She's veggy, feels overweight, *and* The Lizard, her horrible father has just turned up. Worse still, Roy appears – Penny's ex whom she took a year to get over.
ISBN 0 09 985280 2 £2.99

CUTTING LOOSE Carole Lloyd

Charlie's horoscope says to get back into the swing of things, but it's not easy: her Dad and Gran aren't speaking, she's just found out the truth about her mum, and is having severe confused spells about her lovelife. It's time to cut loose from all binding ties, and decide what she wants and who she really is.
ISBN 0 09 91381 X £3.50